# GOLDFIELDS *Girl*

THE *Clara Saunders* STORY

*For Peter Forrestal*
*It's been a long journey*
*Thanks for keeping me company*

# GOLDFIELDS *Girl*

THE *Clara Saunders* STORY

ELAINE FORRESTAL

FREMANTLE PRESS

# AUTHOR'S NOTE

This is a fictional account of the early life of Clara Saunders, based on her own unfinished manuscript, which she called 'Memories'. This handwritten document was mostly recorded in an old exercise book. After her death in 1956, the manuscript was transcribed and the typed pages are now bound and held in the J.S. Battye Library in Perth, Western Australia, under the title *Notes from the Memories of Clara Saunders*, by C. Paton – her married name at the time of her death.

Clara's memories are clear, precise and very detailed. The historical facts contained therein have been verified using material held in the Coolgardie Museum, past issues of the *Coolgardie Miner* and the *Perth Gazette*, the archives of the Eastern Goldfields Historical Society, the Golden Mile Museum and Trove. However, I have at times needed to deviate from the historical facts in the interest of the narrative.

Amongst the many different versions of events in his life that Moondyne Joe himself related, it is almost impossible to sort fact from fiction. I have chosen to use the stories that I find most interesting, but also suit the purposes of my story.

In the case of the well-known bush poet Dryblower Murphy, there is more consistent evidence available, but I have brought his time as a resident of Coolgardie forward slightly to emphasise his friendship with Clara and his importance to the survival of the unique goldfields culture of that time.

I have made every effort to be true to Clara's voice, and for this reason I have used some terms that would be regarded as sexist or racist today, but were part of everyday speech in the 1890s.

While Clara's direct contact with the Wongatha people of the Yilgarn area was minimal, I believe it is significant to her story and shines a light on the wary, but initially tolerant, interactions between two very different groups of people. Sadly these cooperative first contacts did not survive the pressures of the rapidly expanding population of Coolgardie, which by 1901 had become the third largest town in Western Australia.

Elaine Forrestal

# APRIL 1892

'Clara! Come and look.' My sister, Susan, stood at the top of the steps and shouted down from the deck of the steamer to our tiny cabin below.

I turned over in my narrow bunk and pulled the rough wool blanket over my head. I knew the sun was shining outside the porthole, but I didn't want to go up on deck to look at more bare cliffs and deserted beaches. Since we rounded Cape Leeuwin at the end of March we had been travelling north up the coast of Western Australia.

Sometimes we saw sandhills and windblown scrub to our right. At other times there was nothing but endless Indian Ocean.

'Get up, Clara!' Susan was shaking me now, pulling at the blanket while I held it tight. 'We're nearly there!'

I leapt up, threw off the blanket and ran up on deck, wrapping my shawl around me to cover my nightdress. Suddenly there was a terrible clanking sound from the engine below. Our battered steamer gave a great shudder and tipped to one side.

'We're sinking!' Susan screamed, and grabbed the rail with both hands. I was thrown forward and crashed into Mother, who was already there. One of our crewmen leapt off the ship. A moment of panic. Other voices shouting. I was ready to jump when the steamer righted itself and I saw our crewman on the jetty looping a rope around the nearest bollard. He hauled on the rope. Our stern glided slowly towards the Long Jetty and came to rest against a padded pylon. We had finally arrived in the Port of Fremantle.

The jetty was crowded with people coming and going, collecting their luggage, greeting family and friends. There was no-one to meet us. It was much too far for our older sisters, Mary and Emily, to come from Southern Cross, a small gold-mining town 300 miles inland where Mary's husband, Tom Farren, is the licensee of the Club Hotel. It will be eight years in May since Mary married Tom and they left Queensland to try their luck on the new diggings in the west. Emily went with them. I missed her terribly because she used to play games with me, even though I was only six and she was fourteen, the same age as I was now.

Mary was expecting another baby and she needed Mother's help. Not many girls would come and work so far out in the bush. Susan and I were going to help out in the hotel while Mary was laid up after the birth. She and her husband already had four little girls, who we hadn't met yet.

The gangplank slid down and clattered onto the wooden planks of the jetty. We went below to change and get our luggage from the cabin we had been sharing for seven long weeks while the steamer plodded around the coast from our home in Queensland to Western Australia. Mother and I took the handles on either end of our sea trunk and carried it up the steps between us. Susan came behind with our holdalls, one in each hand. As we struggled up to the deck I thought of Pa and our two brothers. I wished they were here to help with the heavy trunk, but I missed them, too. They've stayed behind in Queensland, for now. They all have good jobs at Cooper's Gold Mine, in Charters Towers, and can't afford to lose them.

At the top of the steps, Mother and I rested the trunk on the deck. The steamer's single funnel, its white stripe now coated in grime, had stopped puffing out smoke. After the constant *thump, thump* of the engine, the ship seemed eerily silent, until the captain started barking orders from the wheelhouse and the crew bustled about on deck.

Mother and I lifted the trunk again and carried it down the constantly moving gangplank. Our leather-soled boots slipped and slid on the wet cleats. By the time we stepped onto the jetty I was sweating in my long dress and petticoats.

'Well girls, here we are on dry land at last,' Mother said. Her voice was almost drowned out by the neighing of horses, the shouts of dock workers and the thumps of boxes and bags being loaded into carts and coaches. 'We'll walk to the hotel,' Mother said. 'I believe it's not far, and it will be good to get our land legs back.'

'What about all our things?' Susan bleated, looking at the heavy trunk and holdalls at our feet.

'Just bring your handbag, Susan. I'll arrange for the rest to be delivered,' Mother reassured her.

⁂

Mother found a man with a horse and cart who agreed to take our luggage to the hotel where we would be staying for two days until the next train left for York, the end of the line on the way to Southern Cross.

We were making our way along the busy High Street when suddenly a ragged-looking man came dodging through the crowd. He ran across in front of us, looked back over his shoulder, and knocked a woman off her feet. She fell right in front of Susan, who tripped and grabbed hold of me. I dropped my bag and some of my things spilled out onto the pavement. We heard shouting and the sound of more running feet. A policeman in uniform called out 'Stop him!' People stood and stared, or moved out of the way, but no-one tried to catch the running man, who disappeared into a laneway. The policeman, who was very red in the face, stood on the road with his hands on his hips. He shouted again, but he had obviously given up the chase.

'What's happening?' Mother asked the woman as she helped her to her feet and I began to collect my belongings.

'Oh, one of the prisoners has escaped again,' the woman replied.

'Dear me,' Mother exclaimed. 'Is he dangerous?'

The woman laughed. 'No, not at all,' she said. 'They'll catch up with him and lock him up again, but it will do no good. It's almost a game to them.'

'But what has he done?' I asked the woman.

'All sorts of petty crimes,' she said with a shrug. 'Mostly stealing grog, I believe.'

By then the policeman had recovered his breath and people were going about their business again. Mother handed the woman her bag. She hung it on her arm and wished us a pleasant stay.

We had started to move on when a voice called out behind us. 'Hey miss! You dropped this.' I turned around. A boy about Susan's age was holding up a book. It was an ordinary exercise book, but I could see that it was mine.

# APRIL 1892

The boy handed me the book and I thanked him. It had fallen open at the page I had been writing on. Salty drops of sea water had crinkled the paper and it smelled of oily smoke, but I was glad to have it back. Mother had given it to me when I ran out of books to read early in the journey. Susan and I were only allowed to bring one each. I had read my book of Rudyard Kipling's short stories so many times that Susan agreed to swap with me, but her copy of *Little Women* turned out to be even more boring than staring at the waves sliding endlessly by.

'Why don't you write a story of your own?' Mother had suggested. She lifted the lid of the sea trunk, took out one of her brand-new exercise books and gave it to me. I opened the stiff cover and ran my fingers over the smooth, clean paper inside. I looked at mother.

'Can I write in it?' I asked, feeling the biggest smile pushing up my cheeks.

'Of course, silly girl,' Mother was smiling, too. I threw my arms around her and hugged her tight. 'When I find you a pencil,' she added, extracting herself from my arms and pushing the trunk back against the cabin wall.

With one of Mother's pencils and the exercise book in hand, I climbed up to the deck and sat down on a pile of ropes in the shelter of the wheelhouse.

The sea was so rough I couldn't keep my pencil from wobbling all over the page. Huge swells lifted up our heavy steamer then tipped it into the troughs between each wave. A wall of green water rose up so high it made the steamer seem like a toy boat. It climbed up and up to the top of each wave, balanced there for a moment, then dropped down again with an awful bang. At the bottom it shuddered and shook itself like a dog, before climbing up the next wave. I kept expecting the hull to split apart and hurl us all to the bottom of the sea, but our tough old ship kept ploughing on.

When the weather was calm and the sun shone Mother and Susan came up on deck. Mother sat in the only deckchair and Susan hung over the rail while I continued to write my story.

I wrote about the patterns the clouds were making as they drifted across the sky. And about the sea eagles circling curiously, high above us, then wheeling away towards the coast. They were so beautiful to watch that I was sad to see them go, but it was reassuring to know that Australia was still there, even when we couldn't see it.

Another storm blew up and forced me to go below. Although it was dry inside, the tiny cabin felt as dark and cramped as a coffin. I couldn't help feeling that I would be stuck on that ship for ever. I even imagined falling off the bottom of the world, although I knew that wasn't possible. Before we left Queensland people had told us that Western Australia was a desolate place, all sand, sin and sorrow. By then I didn't care what it was like. I just wanted to get there before we all drowned.

※

I looked up and saw that Mother and Susan had stopped on the street to wait for me. Tucking my exercise book into my bag, I hurried to catch up.

We walked along the streets of Fremantle, admiring the grand official buildings. Between them there were narrow laneways leading to quaint little shops that sold maps and timepieces, ornaments and paintings. A magnificent town hall and a big stone church dominated the high street. Further along, a bustling market sold everything from matches to expensive fur coats.

Mother stopped to buy wool. She had been knitting jumpers for Mary's four little girls and booties for the new baby, but she ran out of wool a week ago. In one of her letters, Mary told us that wool is hard to get in Southern Cross. Sheep don't last long there. It's very dry country and when they run out of food the sheep have to be killed and eaten.

As we passed the post office I saw a postcard with a picture of the Long Jetty and the harbour in the background. I wanted to post it to Mary and Emily, but Mother said it would take three or four weeks to reach them. She said we would be there ourselves in a few days.

※

On our third day in Fremantle, we rode to the railway station in the cart, with all our luggage, and caught the train to York. The train rattled and swayed along the track. I sat with my exercise book in my lap, but I was too busy staring out of the window to write much. There were sheep and cattle grazing on the green hillsides. Trees lined the driveways leading to farmhouses, sheds and barns. It reminded me of Queensland. I thought about Pa and the boys and wondered if Pa was missing us.

⁂

'I wish you were coming with us, Pa,' I had said, standing on the wharf in Brisbane with the steamer blowing smoke and the water slapping against the pylons.

'Don't worry, pet. I'll be joinin' you in the Golden West before you know it,' Pa had said, hugging me tight to his broad chest. Then he lifted me up, swung my feet off the ground and whirled me around in a circle. I'm nearly as tall as him now, but we've played this game ever since I was tiny. I squealed with delight as the wind caught my petticoats and sent them ballooning up above my knees. Susan giggled with her hand across her mouth, but I didn't care. I was enjoying every moment in Pa's arms.

'Take care of your mother,' he said, as he stood me back on my feet and kissed my cheek.

Billy and Joe carried our luggage up the gangplank onto the steamer. Susan and I ran after them, bouncing on the moving boards. Mother followed slowly, turning back for one last look at Pa.

Three mournful blasts from the steamer's blackened funnel sent out a warning to the busy harbour. The two boys hurried back down the gangplank and we pulled away from the wharf. I stood on the deck waving with Mother and Susan, not knowing whether the fluttering in my stomach was caused by excitement or fear. I had never been on a steamer before.

Susan jumped up and down beside me, waving frantically to Pa and the boys. Mother stood gripping the rail, waving her handkerchief then blowing her nose on it, as the men in our family grew smaller and the port faded into the haze.

⁂

The train jerked to a stop and my pencil fell, clattering to the floor. I closed my book and looked out of the window again.

We had arrived in York, but we still had 167 miles to go. Mother had arranged for a buckboard buggy to take us and our luggage the rest of the way to Southern Cross.

'How long will it take?' I asked.

'I don't know,' she said. 'Perhaps three days.'

# APRIL 1892

We bumped along in the buckboard buggy, crammed in with our luggage and all manner of goods that had been ordered by people who live further out beyond York. The road was narrow, the countryside flat and dry with just a few clumps of trees here and there. The buckboard buggy had no roof or sides and the road was very dusty. Whenever we stopped, the cloud of red dust that the horses stirred up swirled all around us. By the end of the day our hair, our clothes, even our eyes and mouths, were full of it.

When the sun started to set we stopped beside the road for the night. Our driver unharnessed the horses and hobbled their front legs together, so that they could eat any grass they could find, but not go too far away.

The camp fire was soon blazing and our driver made tea with pungent leaves and water he carried in a drum specially fitted to the back of the buggy. He took a bucket of water to the horses and hung small bags of hay from each of their bridles.

During the night I woke with a start. I could hear chains clanking and feet scuffling in the dark and imagined a prisoner, escaped from Fremantle, come to rob us of all we had. Then I remembered the horses and laughed silently at myself.

I was just dozing off again when I felt warm breath on my face. I sat up quickly. It was only Susan. Her bed-roll was spread out on the ground next to mine and she had rolled over in her sleep. She was breathing in my ear. The stars were very bright in the dark sky and I was thinking we were lucky it wasn't raining. In the morning I said this to the driver. He smiled.

'No danger of that, miss,' he said, offering me some of the damper he had cooked in the coals of last night's fire. 'Dry as a chip out here.'

⁂

By the time we reached the new wayside inn, all my bones were aching. We had bounced over rocks and ruts, twisted and turned to avoid fallen trees and been shaken about till my brains felt loose in my head. When I finally got down from the buggy, my legs were more wobbly than they had been after seven weeks at sea.

Mary had written about the inn and told us to stay there. Although it was only partially built it would save us going off the main track to the tiny settlement of Doodlakine with its five houses and one water tank.

Mother had arranged for us to spend the night with Mr and Mrs Fred Wilkins, who were building the inn. They had already finished some of the bedrooms and were very pleased to see us.

'Do come in,' Mrs Wilkins said. 'It's lovely to have some female company for once.'

'Thank you,' Mother said.

'We heard that you had passed the crossing. The grapevine is very active out here,' she told us.

I had not seen any grapevines and, in fact, couldn't imagine that anything would grow in the dry, rocky country we had travelled through. Mrs Wilkins took us into an empty room.

'I'm sorry it's so basic,' she apologised.

The walls were made with saplings, obviously cut from the straggly trees nearby. They were roped together and mud was slapped all over the outside to fill the gaps. Part of a corrugated iron roof had been added. The dirt floors had been swept until they were hard and clean.

'It's a struggle to get building materials this far out,' Mrs Wilkins said. 'But we think it will be a good place for an inn. Come and join us when you are settled.'

Once we had spread our bed-rolls on the floor of the room I asked Mother about the grapevines.

'It's just a saying, Clara,' she said. 'In Queensland we called it the bush telegraph.'

I knew about the bush telegraph, of course, but in Queensland people lived closer together and passed on any news or gossip whenever they met. We had just travelled for two days without seeing anyone else on the road, although I did see a cloud of dust away on the horizon. They must have seen our dust behind them and told the Wilkinses.

⁂

Mrs Wilkins cooked a meal for us and afterwards there was lots of singing and laughing. She played her piano accordion and Mr Wilkins started us off by singing 'The Ship that Never Returned'. We all joined in for the chorus. Susan, who has a sweet voice, sang 'I'll Take You Home Again, Kathleen' and Mother sang 'Good Old Jeff'. The driver had lots of jokes and tall tales to tell. I laughed so much I forgot about my aches and pains. It was midnight before anyone even thought of going to bed.

# APRIL 1892

I woke to the harsh cries of magpies, and the sound of them dropping half-eaten gumnuts on the tin roof above my head. It was time to get up and go on our way.

All day we clopped along in the buggy over the dirt road to Southern Cross. The further we went, the more flat, dry and boring the countryside became. Hardly anything moved – except us. A few black cockatoos flew up from a ragged clump of trees. Once we came across a group of kangaroos. They sat perfectly still, staring at us as if we were the strangest creatures on earth. Then they turned and calmly loped away across the plain.

Just before nightfall, we made camp again under the only large tree for miles around. Within minutes the magpies and parrots started shouting at each other – or at us, I'm not sure which. We made a fire and the driver cooked damper. Then we spread our bed-rolls under the stars.

By morning the fire had gone out and every last crumb of damper had been eaten by wild creatures in the night. I could see the black shapes of cockatoos high up in the tree. They sat perfectly still. I stared at them and they stared back with just the odd quick turn of a head or flick of a beak. The wind sighed across the empty plain.

*

We made do with a few dry biscuits and water, boiled the night before, for breakfast. Then we set off again.

As the day wore on the heat became intense. We sat in the buggy with our hats pulled down, our eyes closed and our heads lolling from side to side while the horses plodded on across the sandy countryside. Their pace slowed. Their hooves sank into the loose surface of the track. Once or twice we all had to get down and walk until we reached firmer ground. Then we climbed aboard again and sat dozing and waking by turns. I was convinced we were lost and thought we should turn back.

'Don't be silly, Clara,' Mother said sharply. 'I'm sure the driver knows exactly where we are.'

*

At the top of a rise, the driver called 'Whoa'. The horses stopped and we all sat up. I thought he was going to ask us to walk again. I squinted into the glare. Away in the distance I saw a cluster of buildings. Southern Cross? The driver rested his horses briefly on the ridge and we came down into the town.

As we drew closer, I heard a familiar sound. An unmistakeable *thump, thump, thump*, like a heartbeat, drifted out across the plain and my spirits lifted. It was a sound I hadn't heard since we left Queensland. The sound of a gold mine, the mechanical feet of its hammers stamping away, breaking up the rock to reveal the treasure inside.

Pa had always followed the gold: from our first home in New Zealand, across the Tasman Sea to Victoria; from Bendigo to Ballarat, up into New South Wales, and on to Queensland. When the gold petered out and the mines closed down in one field we moved on to another. 'This time,' Pa would say. 'This time we'll strike it rich for sure!' And we did – sometimes. A nugget here, a panning dish full of colour there. So many small celebrations. Sometimes we were cold and hungry but there were always fish in the streams, rabbits to trap, kangaroos to shoot. Mother planted carrots, peas and silverbeet. Then a new field would be discovered and we would move on again to try our luck on fresh diggings. Gold is in Pa's blood.

*

The main street was full of people.

'There they are!' Mother said. She leaned so far out from the side of the moving buggy that I was worried she would fall as she waved to Mary and Emily. They were already jumping up and down, turning to hug each other, then waving to us again.

The crowd surged forward and I saw four little girls playing hide and seek in and out of legs and skirts. A man who was probably their father was reaching out, trying to catch the children and keep them from running under the wheels of the buggy. Mary and Emily pushed to the front of the crowd of locals who had gathered to collect their long-awaited supplies.

The buggy finally came to a stop and we clambered down into the arms of our family. The children hid shyly behind the adults, staring out at us with big round eyes. There were tears and laughter, hugs and greetings. Mother held both Mary and Emily at once, kissing their wet cheeks, and wiping her own eyes. When she bent down to speak to the little girls, Mary and Emily hugged me and Susan in turn.

Mary took a step back and held me at arm's length. 'Oh, just look at you, Clara!' she exclaimed. 'You are so grown up.'

Emily held Susan's hands. 'Such beautiful girls!' she said. 'The young men about town will have to be beaten off with sticks.'

'I should hope not,' Mother said, trying to sound horrified. But she couldn't stop smiling.

Mary's husband, Tom Farren, searched for our bags amongst the sacks of flour, picks and shovels, parcels and boxes. Mr Farren seemed somehow smaller than I remembered, but he had a jolly face and twinkly eyes.

We thanked our driver for his kindness on the journey, gathered up our belongings and walked across the dusty road to a large, rambling building with a sign that read *Club Hotel*.

'The new extensions are not finished yet, but come and see what we've already done,' Mary said, eager to show us around.

'Let's have a cup of tea first,' Emily suggested. 'You look tired, Mother, and I'm sure Clara and Susan are famished.'

'Of course,' Mary agreed. 'I'm so excited to see you all that I have completely forgotten my manners. Come in to the kitchen and sit down. We are planning a new sitting room, but bedrooms are in such demand we can hardly build them fast enough.'

'I hope we're not putting you out,' Mother said, looking around the large room where one wall seemed to have been knocked out and a wooden bench added.

'Oh, Mother,' Mary cried in dismay. 'We have been so looking forward to you coming, how can you even think that you would be a bother to us?' Mother smiled as Mary hugged her yet again. Tom sent the children outside and dragged extra chairs to the table in the centre of the room. There was a wide fireplace against the outer wall. Two huge pots, suspended on chains, hung above the fire. A stew was bubbling away in one. It smelled wonderful and reminded me how hungry I was. Steam was rising from the other where water was being boiled to make the tea.

The room was hot with the fire on one side and a warm wind blowing in through the open window on the other. It was late afternoon, but I already knew that it would be several hours before the chill of the desert night began to cool the building.

Emily poured the tea. I asked for cold water, but was told that it was not safe to drink unless it had been boiled first. They had run out of rainwater and had to have it carted from a bore outside the town. Mary offered beer and soda from the bar instead. Mother was aghast.

'She's only fourteen,' she said. 'Far too young to be drinking beer.'

‘I know it’s not legal,’ Mary replied. ‘But there are more important things for the police to be worrying about out here.’ Emily stopped pouring for a moment and gave Mary a meaningful look. Mary met her eyes and went on quickly. ‘They understand that sometimes beer is all we have,’ she said.

We drank our tea and ate the griddle cakes that Mary placed on the table. An animated conversation started up again and it was hard to get a word in between Mary and Emily telling us about Southern Cross and Mother enthusing over our visit to Fremantle. Tom had gone back to his work in the bar but the children hovered until Mary gave them a cake each and sent them outside again.

That night we slept in real beds for the first time since we left York.

# MAY 1892

In the morning, Emily showed me around and told me what my new tasks would be.

'You will be looking after Mr Finnerty, and his new wife, doing their beds, their cleaning, their dusting, taking care of everything they need. Mr Finnerty has just been appointed warden for the district. It's a government position, like a magistrate, but he's not at all stiff and starchy. He's a very noble gentleman, and Mrs Finnerty is lovely. You're lucky because they've just moved in to the new suite. Everything is still easy to clean in here.' She gave me a big grin and a reassuring pat on the shoulder, though I didn't need reassuring because really it was not much different from what I did at home. The boys went out to work with Pa each day and I did the chores. Susan was so good at wriggling out of them I got tired of fighting with her. I was always happy when Mother needed me to go with her to deliver someone's baby or patch up their broken bones. Even though she wasn't trained and relied on her 'doctor book', as we called it, people trusted her. She has steady hands and doesn't panic in emergencies.

'It looks lovely,' I said to Emily. 'But don't you find it very dull, living all the way out here?'

'Oh, no,' she said. 'I love it here in the Cross. There are always dances and picnics and singalongs. Everyone is friendly.' Then her face changed. 'We do find it hard to get staff, though. Lots of girls won't come here.'

'Why?' I asked.

She hesitated for a moment. 'Come, let me show you the yard,' she said, and steered me outside. When we were well away from the building she said, 'Mary doesn't like to talk about it and she certainly doesn't want me to mention it to Mother, but the whole town is talking about it. Four weeks ago, Sergeant Williams arrested Baron Swanston for murdering his wife and children, and then his second wife, too. Everyone is in shock. Mr Swanston was the new chief engineer at Fraser's Mine. We have just found out that his real name is Deeming and he was even engaged to be married yet again.'

'Married!' I said.

'Yes. His new fiancée had already started her journey from Adelaide.'

'She's had a lucky escape then.'

'Yes, but how awful to be on your way to a new home and a comfortable life with a chief engineer for your husband, only to find he's a murderer!' At that moment a flock of black cockatoos came screeching overhead, circling the town. Emily shuddered. 'I hope I haven't frightened you,' she said. I shook my head. 'Good. Let's talk about more pleasant things. Are you fond of dancing, Clara?' She asked as we walked back inside.

'Oh yes,' I replied. 'I learned to dance in Queensland.'

'That's wonderful. I'll organise a dance for Monday and introduce you to all the boys.'

*

The next day I started work at the Club Hotel. Mary came with me to the Finnertys' suite of rooms to introduce me to Mrs Finnerty. When Mary introduced me as her sister, Mrs Finnerty took my hand.

'Hello, Clara. It's nice to meet you,' she said. 'I hope you'll be happy here with us.'

'I'm sure I'll be very happy, Mrs Finnerty,' I said, feeling the soft skin of her hands and the warmth of her smile.

'And how old are you?'

'I'm fourteen,' I told her.

'Well, well, I would have taken you to be much older than that. You are a big girl for your age.'

I was a bit put out by that. I'm taller than Susan, but then she is two years younger and fine-boned, like Mother. 'I take after my father, Moroni Saunders,' I said, lifting my chin.

Mrs Finnerty smiled reassuringly and said, 'I'm sure things will work out very well.'

*

True to her word, Emily organised a dance for Monday evening. There would be a band, she said, with piano accordion, banjo and a tin whistle – as long as the musicians stayed sober. A keg of beer would be brought across from the hotel to the Miner's Institute, which had a dance floor in the meeting hall and a small kitchen out the back. Supper would be provided by the women of the town, who were already busy baking biscuits and scones. The men would move chairs, later, and set things up for the evening.

'Now, what are you going to wear?' Emily looked me up and down, measuring me with her eyes.

I only had what Mother called 'sensible clothes' for working in, but Emily pulled out two beautiful dresses from her wardrobe.

'What do you think?' she asked. 'The blue? Or perhaps the apricot?' She held them against me in turn and I clasped them to my waist to check the length. Mary came looking for us and Emily asked her which dress she thought would suit me best.

Mary stood back and tilted her head. 'Hmm … You have such beautiful dark eyes and olive skin, Clara. I think apricot is your colour, don't you Emily?'

'Try it on,' said Emily.

The fabric was so light that the dress seemed to float around me. It was a little shorter than my work clothes and I asked if we should let down the hem, but both Mary and Emily agreed that it looked very stylish and showed off my ankles.

Mary, who is more like Mother and Susan, pulled out one of her dresses for Susan and a lovely skirt for Mother.

'I won't be wearing either of these until after this baby is born,' Mary sighed. Her swollen belly pushed up and out under her apron and she rested her hand on it. I couldn't help staring. 'I'm sure this one is bigger than the others. And more awkward,' she said, taking my hand and placing it on the tight bulge. Even through two layers of clothes I could feel the baby kicking.

'Perhaps it's a boy,' Emily said. They both laughed.

'Boy or girl, I wish it would hurry up,' Mary said, straightening her back and pressing her hands against it to ease the muscles.

*

The Miner's Institute was already crowded. Everyone was dressed in their best clothes with their hair brushed. The sounds of music and laughter greeted us as we carried our plates of food through to the narrow kitchen at the back. The long, wooden bench was already lined with plates, baskets and bowls, all covered by tea towels to keep off the flies that, even after dark, still had an uncanny knack of finding food. An urn bubbled away in the fireplace, heating and sterilising water ready for the inevitable cups of tea that would be served during the interval. A keg of beer rested on its own wooden stand and crates of bottled wine were placed on the floor. Everything had been donated, except these more expensive items which would be covered by the small entrance fee.

We moved into the main hall and sat together on chairs that lined the walls along with the other women. The men stood around in groups. Their hair was neatly brushed, their waistcoats buttoned up and their boots freshly cleaned. They chatted to each other while surreptitiously eyeing off the few young women in the room. When the music started several of the men came across the floor towards us. They obviously wanted to be the first to dance with the new arrivals. It made us feel very welcome.

My first partner was a young man with a charming smile and lively blue eyes. He was a good dancer and I enjoyed every minute of it.

'You waltz well, Miss Saunders,' he said.

'Thank you,' I replied. 'You know my name already?'

A cheeky grin stretched his lips and showed his perfect teeth. 'How could I not?' he asked, twirling me around so that my skirts swung out and lifted above my petticoats. 'I'm Jack Raeside.'

'Pleased to meet you I'm sure, Mr Raeside,' I said, gliding back towards him and matching my steps to his.

'Jack,' he corrected me. Our bodies fitted together again without missing a single beat of the music.

'But we've only just met!' I tried to sound shocked but I could not seem to keep the smile off my face.

'Have we?' he said. 'I could have sworn we had known each other forever.' The music wove some sort of magic as he held me in his arms. I felt a sensation of belonging, of the two of us moving effortlessly together, our bodies gliding across the floor. Then the dance was over. We bowed to each other and he escorted me back to where my mother and sisters were sitting.

I sat down and leaned across to Emily. 'Who is that boy?' I asked.

'Jack Raeside,' she said. 'His father is a very important man. He is in charge of the water supply in the whole of this area. He and Jack have a string of wells and dams they take care of and a team of horses to deliver water to the town.'

The music started again and I danced with a Mr Roberts, but it was not long before Jack was back, asking me to dance with him again.

'I'm sorry, Jack,' I said. Even though he was a much better dancer than Mr Roberts, I felt that it wouldn't be fair. 'I promised I would share my dances. There are so few girls and so many young men.' Jack's face fell so I gave him a reassuring smile.

'I'm disappointed,' he said, looking steadily into my eyes, 'but I do understand.' I watched him walk away to join a group of men standing around the keg.

*

The next evening several of the boys I had met at the dance came along to the billiard room that Tom had set up at the hotel. There was only one table and they had to wait their turn to play. While he was waiting, the accordion player took up his instrument. Soon there was music and singing, clapping and stomping, along with the clack of billiard cues hitting the balls. Lots of voices joined in singing the more well-known songs. After a while someone changed the words, but sang them to the same tune. This brought on a lot of catcalling and laughter. Then it turned into a competition, with others adding new words of their own:

*What shall we do with a drunken miner?*
*What shall we do with a drunken miner?*
*What shall we do with a drunken miner?*
*Earl-i in the morning.*

*Hang him in the washhouse till he's dried out,*
*Hang him in the washhouse till he's dried out,*
*Hang him in the washhouse till he's dried out,*
*Earl-i in the morning.*

Emily arrived with her friend, Tom Scully, who she had introduced to us the night before. Then Jack came over and we all joined in. The rowdy miners swore a lot, but they knew how to sing and harmonise. Time flew and I couldn't believe it when the barman called for last orders. The musicians began to pack up their instruments and everyone talked louder, just to make themselves heard.

'Jack has suggested a riding party to Hope's Hill on Sunday,' Emily said, leaning close to my ear. 'He can bring a horse for you, and Tom will bring one for me. What do you say?'

I hadn't done much riding at all, but I didn't want to miss out on anything. 'That will be lovely,' I said, trying to look confident.

'Good.' I could see that Emily was pleased. I had seen her dancing with Tom Scully the night before and guessed that she wanted to spend time with him – without Mary, or Mother, having to chaperone them. 'Until Sunday, then,' she said to Tom, and let go of his hand. He and Jack turned to go but Jack stopped in the doorway.

'I'll see you on Sunday,' he said, and I noticed again how blue his eyes were and how deeply they looked into mine.

# MAY 1892

Sunday turned out to be a glorious day. The sky was a clear, pale blue above the stark whiteness of the dry salt lake that spread itself out like a field of snow. There was never any snow in Southern Cross, but sometimes, on a winter's morning in Bendigo, the slopes would be white and sparkling and we would make toboggans out of anything we could find and race each other down the mountain.

Jack and Tom arrived at the Club Hotel shortly after breakfast, each mounted on his own horse and leading a spare. Emily and I loaded the food and drinks we were carrying into the saddlebags. Tom got down and held the horse for Emily while she mounted. Jack swung down and stood on the ground holding the head of a large bay gelding. This horse had seemed content to be led with the others until Jack dismounted. Then it started fidgeting, circling around, tangling the lead rope with the reins of Jack's horse.

'Stand up, Buster.' Jack spoke to the gelding and called

me over. 'Buster is one of the best,' he told me. 'He just needs a firm hand at times.'

'I'll remember that,' I said, trying not to sound as nervous as I felt.

I stepped up to Buster's head and reached out to stroke his nose. The horse pulled away and began circling again. Jack calmed him by stroking his neck and feeding him pieces of carrot from his pocket. Buster munched noisily and kept a wary eye on me. His nostrils flared and his ears twitched. He flopped his top lip over another piece of carrot on Jack's hand and scuffled it into his mouth, still watching me.

While Buster was busy chewing, Jack wiped his hands down his trousers, laced his fingers together and held his cupped hands in front of him. I grasped the saddle and put one foot into the cradle of Jack's hands. Energy seemed to flow between us, making me feel strangely light-headed. We stood for a moment, close together, while Jack steadied me, supporting my weight. I took a deep breath to calm my nerves.

'Are you ready?' Jack asked. I nodded, hopping on one foot as Buster tried to move away. Jack lifted me up and I threw one leg over the saddle. When I had settled myself on the horse, Jack adjusted the stirrups, all the while talking quietly to Buster, who was still making small, restless movements.

'Keep him on a short rein at first,' Jack suggested. 'Just until he gets used to you.' Buster nodded his head up and down, but kept his feet still.

We set out across the dry lake at a walk. Buster was inclined to shy at the slightest excuse, but I spoke calmly to him and tried to convince him that I was in control.

'Easy, boy,' I said, and leaned forward to stroke his neck as Jack had done. Buster took this as a signal to trot, which was most uncomfortable, so I decided not to hold him in so tight. I slackened the reins and before I knew it, we were cantering across the firm surface of the lake.

It was exhilarating. The wind cooled my face and arms. I felt my spirits lifting and a great sense of power and freedom filling my body. The horse moved easily into a gallop and we seemed to fly through the wide, uncomplicated landscape. I threw back my head and laughed out loud. Then I glanced behind and saw that the others were a long way back. Reluctantly I decided to slow Buster down. I eased off the pressure of my heels and thighs and pulled back on the reins.

Buster did not slow down. He lowered his head and tossed me forward onto his neck. I clamped my legs more tightly around him but my heels dug into his flank. Now at full gallop, he swerved and turned as if he was trying to throw me off. I grabbed a clump of his mane with one hand. It felt more solid than the flimsy reins. I held on tight.

The sound of another set of hooves came faintly from behind me. Buster twitched his ears. Then, with another great leap, he took off and raced even faster across the plain. The reins hung loose on his neck. I knew I should get them back into my hands but my fingers were clamped in his mane and I was afraid to release them, even for a second. I clung like a leech to the horse's neck with the smell of sweat and leather filling my nose. My hat was long gone and my hair had come loose. Long strands were blowing across my face and into my eyes. Where were the others? A cloud of dust was rising up behind Buster's hooves, blocking out everything behind me. The empty land that stretched ahead was no longer a place of freedom and joy. It had become a potential deathtrap. If I fell, I would be a tiny speck on the vast, undulating plain, lost and alone amongst the spinifex and clumps of scrub that all looked the same. How far back were the others? How long would it take them to find me lying, injured or dead, on the ground?

I clung to Buster for dear life.

# MAY 1892

Suddenly they were with me: Jack lying low on Hunter's neck and Tom behind him, galloping out of the dust cloud.

'Whoa!' Jack shouted. Buster heard his voice. The horse's ears flicked up. His eyes bulged wildly. He laid his ears flat again and dodged away from Hunter's outstretched nose. Jack urged Hunter on and they pulled ahead of us. They wheeled across our path, but Buster was trained to muster cattle and dodged away with ease.

Tom appeared on our other flank. He was shouting for more speed from his horse, Reg, who finally pulled alongside. Tom had looped one of the lead ropes into a lasso. He flung it at Buster's head. The first throw fell uselessly on Buster's neck. It hit my hands and stung my knuckles, but my fingers were still twined tightly in Buster's mane.

Jack brought the galloping Hunter in close. Buster, who was now hemmed in by Hunter on one side and Reg on the other, jerked his head. Tom tried again. The flying noose fell short. Tom gathered it back into his hand and flung it hard and fast. On the next throw the circle of rope fell over Buster's ears.

With the rope tightening on his neck the runaway horse slowed and propped. I was almost thrown from the saddle, but managed to sit up with a jolt. Buster snorted and tossed his head up and down. I gathered the reins into one hand and grabbed hold of the pommel with the other while Jack and Tom brought their horses close so he couldn't get away again.

'That was some ride,' Jack said as he fastened the lead rope to his own saddle. I grinned at him. My face was flushed and wind-burned and my legs were shaking, but I could still feel the excitement of flying across the countryside.

We walked all three horses back towards Hope's Hill. As we got closer, Tom rode on ahead, angling away towards the rise. He had left Emily heading for the well-known picnic spot and was anxious to get back to her.

As Jack and I rode side by side, I noticed a prospector's camp, well away from the others that were clustered together on the edge of the flat plane.

'That's Arthur Bayley's camp,' Jack said when I asked him about it.

'Why does he camp so far out?' I asked, with the memory of the sinister chief engineer, Baron Swanston, still fresh in my mind. 'Is he up to no good?'

Jack laughed. 'Not everyone around here is a murderer, you know. His mate, Will Ford, camps with him. Arthur Bayley has a reputation for being able to smell gold.'

I nodded. 'He finds gold in places where others have walked right by and never noticed it,' I said. Jack looked surprised. 'My Pa was a prospector. I grew up on goldfields,' I explained.

'Ah, so you will know about the claim jumpers who steal other people's finds then,' Jack said.

'Yes, my father and his mates talked about them. But I know nothing about Arthur Bayley.'

As the horses moved rhythmically beneath us, Jack told me how, a few years ago, a prospector named Andy McPherson and an Aboriginal boy called Toobey had staggered out of the desert. They were more dead than alive. Their cheeks were hollow, their tongues black and swollen. Bayley and Ford took them in, gave them food and water, and a place to sleep. When he had recovered enough to talk, McPherson told Arthur they had found plenty of gold out there in the desert, but no water.

'Now the rumours are flying,' Jack said.

'What rumours?' I asked.

'Arthur Bayley is buying horses. We sold three of ours to him yesterday. I reckon he'll be off soon – out bush to look for that gold.'

The low, rocky bulge of Hope's Hill came into view and we saw Emily waving to us. She had spread the picnic rug in the shade of the trees, and set out the food, but had not unwrapped it because of the flies. She and Tom stood waiting for us.

'Everything okay?' Jack asked.

'No sweat,' Tom said, smiling at Emily. 'Very calm, considering her sister had disappeared into the desert on a stranger's horse.'

Emily shrugged. 'I was worried, of course, but what else could I do?' She did look a little pale, nevertheless.

I was shaken by my wild ride, but determined not to show it. When Jack asked if I wanted to go back to town straight away I said, 'What, and miss lunch? I'm starving!'

Jack grinned. He leaned over and took the reins, making sure that Buster stood still while I slid down off his back. He walked both horses over to where Tom had tied the other two in the patchy shade of a gum tree.

Our sandwiches were made from Mother's fresh bread. They were filled with ham cut from the bone, and pickles Mary had made from the small, tough-skinned desert tomatoes. Mother has a saying about hunger making a sauce that will enhance any meal and I believe her. These sandwiches tasted better than any I had eaten before.

Jack teased me about spilling some pickle on my blouse and passed me his handkerchief to wipe it away.

'You were always such a messy baby, Clara,' Emily laughed. 'You never wanted to sit still and eat properly.'

'Mother despaired of me, I know,' I said, and reached for another sandwich.

*

After lunch, Emily and Tom decided to go for a walk. Jack winked at me and we stayed, sipping our billy tea and watching the patterns of light and shade that moved and changed as the breeze swayed the gum leaves high above us.

The afternoon passed too quickly. Jack was interesting to talk to, and I felt so relaxed in his company we could have been old friends. He said he was nineteen, the same age as my older brother Billy, but he was funnier. He made me laugh a lot. We strolled over to the nearby gnamma holes where the Aborigines come for water. He carefully lifted some of the bark and leaves that covered one of the holes. The water underneath looked brown and undrinkable.

'It's only good for washing in, unless you boil it,' Jack said. 'But when the rains come it will be clear and sweet.' He and his father knew a lot about water and had great respect for the Aborigines who had shown them where to find it in their harsh, dry country.

In the cool of the evening, Emily and Tom came back and we all rode slowly into town. The horses walked in pairs while we chatted to each other. The dramas of the day were already receding into the pattern of outback life. As we rode, Jack and I sometimes lapsed into long, comfortable silences and I realised how much at home I felt with him. Even though we had only known each other for such a short time, I already had a feeling that he would be an important part of my life.

# MAY 1892

Though they had tried to be careful to conceal their movements, word got around that Arthur Bayley and William Ford had left town the next day. Rumour had it that they had taken five horses and provisions for three months, plus equipment for digging, pegging and carrying gold. No-one was particularly surprised, since prospectors were always coming and going – mostly going. Speculation about new finds flared and died as often as their camp fires, but Bayley and Ford would have to keep their wits about them if they did strike colour.

⁂

A few days after the picnic, a strange old man came into Southern Cross. He was tall and gaunt with weathered skin and a shaggy beard. His dungaree trousers were tied up at the waist with a faded red scarf. Corks hung from the brim of his hat to keep the flies away. He had a dog with him, which was long-legged and scruffy but seemed healthy enough. We passed in the street and his dog stretched out its nose to sniff me.

'Here, boy,' the man muttered, without looking up.

'It's all right,' I told him, putting out my hand to pat the dog. 'I'm not afraid.' The man lifted his head and stared at me with piercing grey eyes. Then he staggered on down the street, using the long stick he carried to steady himself.

I finished my errand and went back to the hotel. The same man was now sitting at the bar with two empty beer glasses on the counter and his dog at his feet.

Tom Farren came out to the kitchen to help me put away the new supplies.

'Who is that man in the bar?' I asked him.

'That's Moondyne Joe, the famous bushranger,' he told me.

I'd never met a real bushranger, even though I'd heard lots of stories about men like Ned Kelly and Captain Moonlite. Pa told me not to believe everything I heard. Those tales would become more incredible each time they were told, he said, as if each storyteller had to outdo all the others.

True or not, I still liked to imagine myself on a fine black horse leaping over fallen trees, escaping from the police with my haul of gold, travelling all over the world and never wanting for anything ever again.

I leaned across to get a glimpse of the man through the open door. 'He looks exhausted,' I said.

'He's probably walked into town. His camp is about six miles out,' Tom said. 'And he's not getting any younger.'

⁕

A week later I saw Moondyne Joe again. He was sitting in the shade of a tree, resting his back against the trunk. His dog lay stretched out beside him and a group of children clustered around.

'Hello again,' I said. The dog opened one eye, but didn't get up. 'Do you mind if I sit here?'

A boy with a grubby face moved closer to Joe and I sat down in his place. There were two other children: a girl with a mass of tight curls, and a younger boy who sat in front of Joe. They stared at me curiously.

'I'm Clara Saunders,' I said, and held out my hand. 'I'm Mrs Farren's sister.'

'Oh,' Joe said, ignoring my hand. 'I suppose they've told you all about me then.'

'Well, no. Not really. In any case I like to make up my own mind about things – no matter what other people tell me.'

Joe said nothing, just stared silently into the distance, until the girl said, 'Come on, Joe, finish the story.'

'You know, I've never really done any really bad crimes,' Joe said, looking directly at me.

'How come you were in gaol, then?' the girl asked.

'I've never killed or wounded anyone, or ever molested a woman. In my young days I was a lock picker – the best in England. I could pick the tightest lock,' Joe said proudly, lifting his chin.

'One day I was in a tavern with three friends. We were drinking together and they made a bet with me. They bet that I couldn't get into a certain mansion in London. It was a fair amount of money they were offering. I told them they would lose their money.

‘That night I got into the mansion. Right into the lady’s apartment. But I heard someone coming and hid under the bed. Sadly I was discovered and arrested for trespassing.’

‘Did they slap you in irons?’ asked the bigger boy, his eyes lighting up.

‘A lot of people wanted to see me flogged,’ Joe continued. ‘Some said I should be hanged. That made me look bad, but the men who had made the bet, they stood very loyal by me and told the magistrate that it was their idea and that I hadn’t meant to harm anyone or steal anything from the lady.’

The children sat staring at Joe, waiting for more.

‘While the long arm of the law was making up my sentence,’ Joe went on, ‘two men came to me and asked me to open a safe for them. They were well-dressed gentlemen and when I said, “Why don’t you use the key?” they said, “We’ve tried that. We’ve tried duplicate keys as well, but the lock is jammed tight and there are important documents inside. If you open this safe for us we’re sure your other crime will be overlooked.”

‘Well, I was happy to open their safe and recover their documents,’ Joe paused to push his hat back and wipe his forehead with the back of his hand. ‘I did escape being put in prison, but I was lagged out to Western Australia instead.’

‘What’s “lagged out”?’ the smaller boy asked. Joe hesitated and looked slightly embarrassed.

‘I believe it means sent out here as a convict,’ I prompted.

‘But not now, I’m not,’ Joe declared fiercely. ‘I got me ticket of leave, I have. I’m a free man.’

'Tell us about stealing the policeman's horse,' demanded the bigger boy.

'And the way you just kept on escaping from Fremantle Prison,' the girl laughed.

'Yeah, tell us!' the others chorused.

Joe was silent again. He seemed to be thinking deeply about something. His hand went automatically to his dog's head, as if for reassurance, before he spoke.

'It embittered me to be called a lag,' he said. 'And that policeman, he had it in for me. But he couldn't catch me. Oh no. No-one could catch me. I hid out in Moondyne Gully. I lived off the land, mostly, but sometimes I got thirsty and stole a few bottles of grog from the trader in Toodyay.' Joe's head was nodding and his eyes were closed. I wondered if he was dropping off to sleep, but he straightened his shoulders. 'That's where the nickname, Moondyne Joe, comes from.'

'And when you pinched the horse you took it back to Moondyne Gully and ate it!' The older boy laughed so much he fell on his back in the dirt.

'Ah, yes. They got me for that one. But they couldn't keep me in gaol. They got tired of having to find me and lock me up again, so the Governor of Western Australia says to me, "Joe, if you escape again I swear I'm just going to leave you roaming."' Joe gave a gravelly laugh and his eyes crinkled at the corners. 'He didn't believe anyone could get out of that tiny cell he'd had built specially for me. I'm smarter than that, you know. They couldn't send me outside the prison walls to work off me sentence. They knew I'd get away, quick smart. So they brought in a pile of rocks for me to split inside the prison walls. Only I split their wall for 'em, instead.' He laughed heartily at this, slapping his knees and rocking his body. 'I went about it careful, mind, so they wouldn't notice. Bit by bit, I made a hole behind the pile of rocks. Then one day I just slipped through. I made up a scarecrow and dressed it in me prison garb so they thought I was still working!' He was laughing so hard that his eyes watered.

'After that, I took to the bush. And the new governor, he let me be.' Joe patted the dog. It raised its eyes.

'Michael! Paddy!' A woman's voice was calling. 'Come on home, now. Yehs best get yer chores done or yer da'll be after ye.' The two boys sprang up and the girl ran after them, even though she hadn't been called.

'Bye.'

'See you later, Joe,' they shouted, and ran off with the red dust kicking up behind their bare feet.

When they had gone, I turned back to Moondyne Joe. 'You have certainly had an interesting life,' I said. 'I hope you will tell me more about it, next time you come to town.'

He didn't reply and seemed to have retreated into his own thoughts again. I stroked his dog's ears and left them both sitting there in the fading light.

I returned to the hotel to find Emily looking for me.

'At last!' she said. 'I was about to take the Finnertys' dinner tray to them myself.'

'Sorry,' I said. 'I was listening to Moondyne Joe.'

'That explains it,' Emily said. 'He'll tell tales till all the cockies have come in to roost, but who knows if they're true. Sometimes I think he makes them all up – except the one about being sent out here as a convict. That one seems to stay the same. Here.' She handed me a tray, already loaded with two plates of food covered by a tea towel, knives and forks wrapped in linen serviettes, a bottle of wine and two glasses. 'Mind how you go.'

# SEPTEMBER 1892

It was 16 September 1892 when Arthur Bayley finally rode back into Southern Cross.

I noted the date because Susan and I had been writing letters to send to Pa and the boys. Susan had asked Mother which date to put at the top of her letter, but Mother wasn't sure and had to check. No-one in Southern Cross worried too much about the exact date, or even what time it was. Life progressed at its own pace. The pub was open, or it was not open. The dancing had begun, or it was about to begin. The sun was rising into a clear, blue sky, or setting like an orange cut in half by the horizon. I was never bored. There were singalongs and picnics, parties and racing carnivals. Everyone came. If you hadn't already been told all the details, or read the posters around town, you just asked someone at the hotel.

I had finished my work in the Finnertys' suite and was dusting around the reception area while it was quiet after the lunch rush. It was a thankless task. A coating of fine red dust rose from every surface, and promptly settled again as soon as I turned my back. If the dusting wasn't done every day, though, things quickly changed colour and felt gritty to touch.

I became aware of someone else in the room and looked up to see a man standing at the counter. Two battered leather saddlebags lay at his feet.

'Do you have any rooms?' he asked, taking off his hat and looking towards the bar where bottles glinted invitingly on the shelves and glasses hung upside down in the wooden racks above.

'I'll go and get Mr Farren,' I said. The man wiped dust and sweat from his forehead. His brown eyes were dull with fatigue.

I hurried to find Tom.

*

'A single room, is it Arthur?' Tom asked, reaching for the hotel register and placing it open on the bar. The man wrote his name, Arthur Bayley, and booked the room for two nights. When the paperwork was completed, Tom asked me to show Mr Bayley to his room while he went outside to take the horse around to the stables. By the state of his clothes and boots, it looked like Arthur Bayley had ridden a long way. When he picked up his bags from the floor, he staggered a little under their weight.

'Mr Farren will bring your bags to the room for you,' I explained. 'He will be back in a few minutes.'

'I'll carry them,' Mr Bayley said. 'They're not heavy.'

He saw the questioning look on my face, but made no further comment.

His room was one of the newer ones at the back of the hotel. I walked ahead of him, but had to slow down as he stopped every few seconds to rest the bags on the ground. When we reached the room I opened the door and he looked all around it, into the corners and under the bed.

'Is everything to your liking?' I asked, indicating the china bowl and jug on the bedside table and the hanging rail that stretched across one corner.

'Yes,' he said. 'But please tell Tom that I don't want to be disturbed.'

'Certainly,' I said. 'Dinner is served from eight o'clock onwards.'

'I won't be eating dinner, thank you. I'll be sleeping.'

I looked at his face, still covered in grime, except for the paler strip where he had wiped his forehead. I was about to explain that water cost two shillings a gallon, but he waved me away and closed the door.

⁂

By ten o'clock the next morning, the town was buzzing with the news. Arthur Bayley had put 554 ounces of pure gold on display at the Commercial Bank and registered a claim in his own name and that of his mate, William Ford, who had stayed behind to stand guard over their find. The whole town was alive with rumours. The reef was three feet wide and fifty yards long. No, three feet above ground and sixty yards long. It was a hundred yards long with veins of gold as thick as your finger, all shining in the sun! There were so many different stories, but one thing was clear. This was a reef of gold to rival any in the world. A sight for sore eyes. The stuff of dreams. Bayley and Ford had struck it rich. They could claim the reward, offered to anyone who found a new field, and live like kings for the rest of their lives.

*

When lunch was over, I crossed the road to see for myself. A crowd of people still clustered around the display. The magnificent collection of pure gold nuggets winked and glinted on a black cloth spread on the counter. Mr Bayley, with his pistol in full view, stood guard over his stash. His freshly washed face was beaming as he answered questions and described the enormous ridge of gold he and Ford had found.

'What you see in front of you, gentlemen, is a tiny fraction of the whole,' he said. 'A few nuggets broken off from the main reef, which is almost a mile long.'

'How wide?' someone shouted from the back of the growing crowd.

'In my estimation, about twenty feet wide and in some parts rising above the flat plain to a height of …' Arthur Bayley paused to calculate, '… say three feet, maybe a little more.'

The buzz of voices increased. 'You're havin' a lend of us, ain't ya?' one shouted.

'Yeah, wantin' some sucker to buy youse out,' another grumbled.

Arthur Bayley stood calmly, his eyes scanning the crowd. 'Believe that if you wish,' he said. 'The evidence is here before you.'

Men began to leave the room. Others arrived. The disbelief on their faces quickly turned to amazement.

I stared at the knobbly rocks, all shining with rich, golden colour. To me they were unbelievably beautiful. Here was my father's lifelong dream. The elusive treasure. The gold that he loved and cursed, but could never quite give up searching for. The thought of it lying out there in the desert, undiscovered for thousands, maybe millions of years made the hairs stand up on my neck. If only Pa had come with us. He and the boys would not be breaking their backs in the dark pits and narrow shafts of Cooper's Mine. They would be packing up their picks and shovels, like everyone else, and heading out to the new diggings. A reef like Arthur Bayley was describing would not be lying out there on its own. There was obviously a lot more gold in the area, still to be found.

I don't know how long I had been standing there, mesmerised, before I noticed the crowd was gone. I was the only one left. Arthur Bayley sat alone on the high stool next to the counter.

'Excuse me, Mr Bayley.' He turned in my direction. 'People are saying you camped for the night by a rocky pool. But everyone says there's no water out there in the desert.'

'True,' he said. 'But on the way out we had seen a group of blacks sitting around in the shade of some rocks. We kept moving, but our water was on the low side by sundown so we decided to go back there and camp nearby. It turned out to be a rock pool that still held seven or eight hundred gallons of water from the rains we had about a month ago.

'In the morning I got up early to catch the horses and picked up a half-ounce slug. It was lying in a boot print.'

‘What? Someone had trodden on a half-ounce gold nugget and didn’t even notice it?’ I couldn’t believe that anyone could be so blind, even if the nugget was covered in dirt.

‘Yep,’ Arthur Bayley said. ‘We reckon it must have been that surveyor chap who was working out there for Hampton Plains Company a while back.’

‘And the reef?’ I asked.

He smiled and his eyes lit up. ‘First bit of gold we saw on the reef was a great yellow blotch on the face of the stone. It was nice to look at and we didn’t touch it. But we couldn’t sleep for fear of someone turning up and noticing the nuggets lying around. Will has his revolver and my horse is faster than his, so he stayed on guard while I came in to register the claim. I have to be getting back, though. Good day to you, miss.’

I stepped outside. The usually quiet street was packed with people. It was hard to believe that this was the same town I had lived in for the last three months. The men were calling to their friends, hugging their wives and children, gathering up anything they might need, everything they could carry. They were all heading out of town in the same direction. Heading for gold. Every horse, wagon, cart and wheelbarrow was being loaded to the top with shovels, picks, waterbags and tents. Men were leaving in pairs, in groups, on their own, while their womenfolk clustered together. The women’s faces were set. They were preparing, in their own way, for the hard times to come. They knew it was no use trying to hold their menfolk back. They recognised gold fever when they saw it.

# SEPTEMBER 1892

Jack did not go with the men. His father needed him to run the team of horses that delivered water to the Cross. I had already made other friends in the town, but Jack was my best friend. He was cheeky and full of surprises. The same things made us laugh and we both loved dancing. Although we danced with other people during the evening, we made a habit of saving the first and last dances for each other. Afterwards we would often go for a stroll out to the ridge above the town. Emily and Tom sometimes came with us, at least part of the way.

'Are you thinking about trying your luck on the new field?' I asked Jack one night, as we sat staring up at the vast black sky full of stars.

'What, and risk you finding a better dancing partner while I'm away?' he said.

'That's not likely,' I told him. 'All the boys in town have either gone, or they're packing up to go. They say there are already more than two thousand men camped out there at Bayley's Reward. And Mr Wisdom has gone out there to build a new hotel. I heard he's ordered six water tanks and they're already on their way from Perth.'

'Are they now?' Jack said. 'And where does he plan to get water to fill his tanks?'

I already knew that the soaks and waterholes in the area were nearly dry. And the camel teams going through to the new diggings had fouled what little water was left. A few of the Aboriginal gnamma holes still had water in them, but that wouldn't last long amongst two thousand thirsty prospectors.

Water was never a problem on the diggings in the east. There were always streams or rivers nearby so we carried our own water up to the hut in buckets. Out here in the desert, water could be harder to find than gold. Jack's father had signed a contract to deliver water to the new diggings regularly, by horse and dray, from the soaks and wells he owned. A purifying plant had been set up in Southern Cross to supply the town when the surface water ran out, but the new diggings were more than a hundred miles from anywhere. It would take at least three days to reach them.

'Will you and your father cart water out to them?' I asked, already planning to go there, if I ever got the chance. How exciting it must be to pick up nuggets off the ground, without having to dig, or even pan for them.

'There's no road at all out there yet,' Jack said, shaking his head. 'Although with so many people trekking across the country, there'll soon be wheel tracks to follow.'

'Jack!' I suddenly had an idea. 'What if you, or your

father, picked up a nugget on one of your delivery runs? I know Pa would be off to try his luck the minute he heard about something like this.'

Jack looked at me thoughtfully. 'Sometimes I do think about being rich,' he said. 'But I don't want to die of thirst.'

'There must be a way to have water and gold,' I insisted.

'Come on,' Jack said. 'Wave your magic wand, then.'

'Abracadabra!' I leapt up and waved an imaginary wand over his head. 'Oh look. You've turned into a frog,' I teased.

'Cr-o-a-k,' he gasped, clutching his throat. He did a funny frog jump towards me and I started to run. 'Come back here and undo this spell,' he called, and chased me until we were both out of breath.

'No-o,' Jack moaned as we stood together, breathing hard and looking across to the darkened town. 'It's too late! The witching hour has passed. Now I'll be a frog forever.'

The hotel lamps were put out at midnight. The town was in darkness.

'Never too late to undo a wrong, my mother says. Anyway, I don't want a frog walking me home.'

'So you agree to release me from your spell, then?' Jack asked.

'Just for now,' I conceded, and linked my arm through his.

⁂

As we walked back to the hotel I thought about the differences between Jack and me. His family valued water above most things, but gold had an unbreakable hold on mine. Even when Pa did strike it rich, it didn't satisfy him for long.

'This is just the beginning!' he would say, showing us the nuggets in his hand. 'There's more colour out there. I can feel it in me bones.' Chasing the gold wasn't such a problem for him. Water and gold go together in the east. Here we seem to have one or the other, but not both.

We usually lived in a tent on the diggings, outside the towns, until we could build a hut. Pa and the boys hunted rabbits and wallabies for food. Mother cooked over the open fire. It was a new adventure for all of us children. We had our chores to do, but once they were done we were free to explore, play games, make up stories. Mother taught us reading and writing – and good manners, of course. She was very strict about that. When there was gold to take to the bank, we went into the nearest town with Pa. There were shops with real windows and they sold iced buns for a penny each. The icing on top came in lovely colours. I could never decide which to have.

'I wish we could live in the town,' Susan said once.

'No, you don't!' Billy told her.

'I do!' Susan protested. 'We could have iced buns every day.'

'Shush!' Joe said, giving her a poke. Mother and Pa were just up ahead. 'We'd have to go to school every day, stupid.'

'Come along now,' Mother called, looking around to see what the fuss was about.

I grabbed Susan by the hand and tugged her along. By then I'd had enough of the noisy town and its smelly drains.

Southern Cross only smells of salt and dust, but I'm getting a bit tired of it. The big adventures of our sea voyage and even my first ride in a buckboard buggy seem so long ago now. The excitement of seeing Mary and Emily again has worn off, too. Meeting Mary's four little girls has been fun – although Mother is much more interested in them than I am. I wonder if my wild ride out into the desert on Buster has woken something inside me. A hankering for the freedom that is missing in the towns, a need for new adventures, different challenges perhaps?

*

Over the next few days the last of the prospectors filtered out of the town and Jack got ready to make his first run to the new diggings. When I had finished my work on the day Jack was due to leave, I went down to the Raeside stables. He was still loading up his wagon.

'I've decided to stick to carting water,' Jack said.

'Why?' I asked.

'Because … Well, because water is life, isn't it?'

'But someone else could cart it, couldn't they?' I was not looking forward to Jack being so far away for at least six days at a time.

'My father can't do everything.'

Jack finished the loading and we sat on the buckboard together. The wind sighed around us as if we were in its way. It lifted the brim of Jack's hat, flapped at my skirts and blew my hair into my eyes. I thought of all the creatures who lived out there in the desert and wondered how they managed without water. At least they didn't have to cook and clean and wash their clothes in it.

'They're calling the new town Coolgardie,' Jack said, breaking the silence that had stretched out and settled over us like a bedsheet. 'It's a name the natives use for mining areas. It means "white man's holes".' He gave a half-laugh. With that look in his eyes I was never quite sure whether he was joking or not.

'Really?' I asked.

'Dinky-di. Cross my heart –' I quickly put my hand over his mouth. I didn't want him to say the rest of the old rhyme, but he pulled my hand away. 'And hope to die,' he said, still holding my hand. Then he thought again. 'Better not, eh? If I die who'll drive the team to Coolgardie?'

'Not me,' I said. 'I couldn't.'

'I bet you could,' Jack said. 'If you put your mind to it.'

# OCTOBER 1892

A week after Jack made his first water run to Coolgardie, we moved out of the Club Hotel and into an empty house that Mother had rented. When the first knock came on our front door I wondered whether it was someone looking for us, or for the people who lived in the house before.

I opened the door to find Mr Wisdom standing there. Unlike the miners and prospectors in town, he was always neat and well dressed. He had been the licensee of a hotel in Southern Cross, before he moved out with the new rush. He was back in town because his housekeeper, Mrs Fagan, was finding it difficult to cope. He had put advertisements in the *Perth Gazette* and was asking around the town for someone to come and work for him. When I heard Tom telling Mary I said I would love to go, but Mary was horrified so I said no more about it. I found it difficult to ignore a sort of buzzing in my stomach, though. As if this was my big chance, right here on our doorstep.

‘Good morning, Clara,’ Mr Wisdom said, lifting his bowler hat to me. ‘Is your mother in?’ It was a small house and the front door opened straight into the sitting room. Mother had heard his voice and was, by then, close behind me.

‘Do come in, Mr Wisdom,’ she said. ‘Would you care to sit down?’

Mr Wisdom sat down in the only armchair. I quickly brought a straight-backed chair from the kitchen and placed it opposite. Mother sat in it and I went back to the kitchen to boil the water and make tea. I stayed out of sight but I couldn’t help hearing Mr Wisdom explaining to Mother that his new hotel in Coolgardie was being swamped by men needing rooms. And that he had not been able to persuade anyone to go out and work in the new settlement. ‘I was wondering if Clara would be interested?’

‘Oh dear,’ Mother said. ‘We would like to help, but Clara is busy here –’

At that point I completely forgot my manners and burst into the sitting room. ‘I’m not busy, Mother,’ I declared. ‘I would love to go to Coolgardie.’

Mother’s mouth opened, but no sound came out so I grabbed my chance.

‘I can cook and clean. I am strong and will work hard for you, Mr Wisdom. I have had some experience, looking after the warden and Mrs Finnerty. I know I can do the job.’

Mr Wisdom studied me closely. ‘How old are you, Clara?’

‘I’m fourteen,’ I said proudly.

He paused and considered this for a moment, then he said, 'Well, I was looking for someone a little older, but …'

'Were you indeed?' Mother said. There was a different tone to her voice. One that I knew well. I had learned not to cross her when she used it. 'Clara is young, but very capable, Mr Wisdom,' she said firmly. 'And completely trustworthy.'

Mr Wisdom looked quite taken aback. 'But, are you not worried about her travelling all the way to Coolgardie – on her own? We cannot afford to pay wages for more than one person.'

'Clara loves travelling,' Mother insisted. 'Believe me, Mr Wisdom, she is a strong young woman and can take care of herself.'

Mr Wisdom lowered his eyes in the face of this challenge. Mother continued to look steadily at him, but I saw a familiar tilt to her eyebrows. I could hardly contain my excitement, but knew that I must be careful. Mother approved of self-confidence, but it must never take the place of good manners. This was always a delicate balancing act and I did not want to damage my chances. I could hear the water boiling in the kitchen and decided this was the moment to go and make tea.

I wanted to make a good impression on Mr Wisdom, so I carefully arranged a tray with tea in the pot, a small bowl of sugar and two cups on matching saucers. I placed the tray on the upturned box beside the chair where Mr Wisdom was sitting. Mother had spread a colourful cloth over the box and we used it as a table. I poured tea for Mr Wisdom. He took it from me, sat forward in the chair and lifted the cup to his mouth.

'I believe that you and your family have lived on the goldfields of every colony in the country,' Mr Wisdom said, taking a sip of the hot, black tea.

Mother gave a short laugh as I poured her tea and handed it to her. 'Perhaps we do have some gypsy blood in us,' she said. 'But we are a versatile and hard-working family.'

'You are indeed,' Mr Wisdom said. He sipped his tea and leaned back in the chair. 'And since I have not been overwhelmed by people interested in the position, I will accept Clara's application.'

My hands flew up to my hot cheeks. It was all I could do to stop myself from jumping for joy. I put my arms around Mother and hugged her. Then I remembered my manners and thanked Mr Wisdom for his kind acceptance.

'My pleasure,' he said, and extended his hand. I shook it firmly. 'Snell's coach leaves at seven o'clock on Monday morning. Can you be on it?'

'Yes, sir,' I nodded, and held my breath to contain my excitement.

When I returned to the kitchen Susan was there. Her face was ashen. 'You're never going to leave us, Clara,' she said.

'I am! I am! Can you believe it? I will be earning my own money, making my own way in the world. Maybe I will even find some gold, like Pa.' Susan looked as if she was about to cry. 'Oh, Susan,' I said. 'You can come and visit. You can all come and visit me in my new home. It will be so exciting!' I did a little dance around the kitchen table.

Mother came back from seeing Mr Wisdom out and I hugged her again. 'Thank you, thank you,' I said.

‘I hope you will still be thanking me in a year’s time,’ Mother replied with a doubtful smile. ‘But I will not have any man thinking we are less capable than he is. I hope I have at least brought you all up to be practical and self-reliant.’ She looked at Susan, then back to me.

‘You have, you have,’ I said enthusiastically. ‘You won’t regret it, Mother. I promise.’ I just couldn’t stop smiling.

# OCTOBER 1892

When I told Jack outside the Club Hotel that night, his mouth fell open and he almost swallowed a fly. 'Clara, you can't be serious!' he spluttered.

'Why not?' I had expected him to be pleased for me, at the very least. 'It will be a great adventure,' I told him. 'I can't wait to see Bayley's Reward for myself. They say the great reef is sticking up out of the desert, with chunks of gold catching the sunlight. It's like a sleeping giant, with its clothes and hair all speckled with gold. The biggest reef of gold in the world! So they say.' I wanted Jack to be as excited as I was, but he sat there with a face like a thundercloud.

'You know what men are like, Clara – they exaggerate,' he said. 'One tells a tall tale, sitting by the camp fire, and the others have to tell an even taller one, just to go one better.'

'But you saw the gold at the bank,' I reminded him.

'That could have come from anywhere,' he said.

'Jack.' I took his hand. 'I know you think I'm dreaming, but I've lived out in the bush before. And I've been around miners and prospectors all my life.'

'Yes, but the desert is different. It's totally unforgiving. Food is scarce and the water situation out there is desperate. My father has just come back from an inspection. Levels in the wells and soaks are all low. They smell bad and there's a plague of flies. He says that if Warden Finnerty can't do something about it quickly there will be terrible epidemics. Some of the men in the camps have already died from dysentery and typhoid. Those diseases spread like wildfire in crowded places with no facilities. I've seen men coming in from new diggings looking like the walking dead. Their eyes are vacant, their tongues so swollen they can't speak. On his last inspection rounds my father found three skeletons at the bottom of a dry soak out there. Human skeletons.' Jack paused, making sure I was getting the full impact of his words. 'They had an empty billy between them and it looked like they'd tried to write their names, on claim pegs, in their own blood. The weather had all but wiped away the writing and he couldn't make out who they were.'

I stared at him, wondering if it was true. But this was my big chance to be independent, to make my own way in the world. 'Others have faced it. Why can't I?' I said with my hands on my hips.

'I just don't think you have thought this through,' Jack said. 'What if there's an emergency? You'll be at least three days from any medical help. You'll only have Mrs Fagan for company. Just the two of you and two thousand rowdy, drunken, violent men!'

He looked so worried that I laughed at him and gave him a dig in the ribs. 'Jack Raeside, I do believe you're jealous.'

That made him smile. 'Of course I am,' he said. 'Who am I going to dance with, once you're gone?' He put one arm around my waist and we did a few waltz steps. We tried to twirl but the loose stones slipped under our feet. I grabbed the front of his shirt to stop myself from falling. His button popped off and the strap of my pinafore slipped down my arm. We staggered and tried to straighten up. When we looked at each other we burst out laughing.

Inside the hotel, dinner was over. Customers were emptying out in twos and threes, wending their way home to their families. When they saw us they stopped to call out 'Cheerio', or made jokes about us dancing in the street. We laughed some more and returned their greetings.

When we were alone again I said, 'I know how you feel about me going, Jack. We've been such wonderful friends and I will miss you. But this is my big chance.'

The laughter had gone from his eyes. 'Well,' he said, resigning himself, 'if I can't change your mind, I'll just have to deliver water to Coolgardie more often, to keep an eye on you.' He forced a smile and patted my hand.

'I don't need a nursemaid!' I protested. 'But I expect there will be dances there, the same as here. You'll have to wait your turn, though – like before.' I gave a little skip of excitement and said goodnight.

# OCTOBER 1892

I was impatient to be off on my new adventure, but as the time to leave came closer a sudden sense of loss washed over me. I would be leaving my mother, my sisters, the friends I had made here. Jack was right – Mrs Fagan, who was much older than me, would be my only female companion. I tried to put these thoughts out of my mind. Fortunately there was still a lot of work to be done. Mother fussed about my clothes. Emily cooked and filled a whole tin with biscuits that would withstand the heat and last for many weeks. Susan gave me a set of writing paper and envelopes that she had bought in Fremantle.

'I've only used a few from this pack so they will last you nearly a year,' she said. 'You will write every week, won't you?'

'Of course I will,' I said, knowing how much she treasured this smooth white paper and feeling surprised that she was willing to part with any of it at all. 'I promise

I'll write and tell you everything. Jack can bring the letters back to you, each time he carts water to Coolgardie.'

I hadn't written in my exercise book lately. I told myself I was too busy living my life to write about it. Sometimes there was nothing much to say, but that would change. I knew life was about to become a whole lot more interesting.

'Clara,' Mother was calling from the sitting room. I found her standing by the wooden box that held our small collection of books. 'I want you to take this. Keep it by you and consult it whenever you feel the least bit poorly.' She held out a thick, well-thumbed book. The words *Encyclopaedia of Common Diseases and Remedies* were written on the cover. I recognised it instantly. It had been a standby of hers and I had seen her consult it often. Not just when one of our family was feeling unwell. There were very few doctors in the places where we lived. My mother's combination of intelligence, common sense and her encyclopaedia meant that people sought her out in an emergency. Over the years, she had helped many people recover from illnesses, broken bones and difficult births.

'But Mother, what will you do without it?' I asked.

'I will order another one,' she said. 'I have heard that diseases like scurvy and dysentery – even typhoid – are rife amongst the prospectors on the new field.' She handed me the book and I clutched it to my chest. There was such a comforting weight to it and the marks of my mother's hands were all through its pages. I placed it carefully inside my bag and hugged her. She held me close. 'Please be careful, Clara.' Her voice was steady but gentle in my ear.

⁂

By Monday morning I was ready to go. Tom and Mary, Emily, Susan, Mother and Mrs Finnerty all came to say farewell and to see me safely onto Snell's coach. Jack was already out loading water at one of the wells, sixty miles away.

Mr Snell, who was a licensee at the same hotel as Mr Wisdom, liked to drive the coach himself. He sat in the driver's seat, in his workboots and battered hat, and held the reins of the two harnessed horses who stamped and snorted their disapproval of all the tears and fluttering handkerchiefs.

'Good luck, Clara,' Tom said. His eyes and mine were the only dry ones in the group, although I did have a strange lump in my throat as I waved my last goodbyes.

There were four other passengers travelling to Coolgardie that day, all hoping to strike it rich on the new find. A man called Jock, who wore a tartan waistcoat, was taking first turn at sitting up on the driver's bench with Mr Snell. The rest of us sat inside the coach. Harry and his brother Will, both with black curly hair and beards, sat on the bench seat opposite. They were introduced by Tom Farren's mate, Mac, who sat beside me.

⁕

We set off at a good fast pace in perfect weather. The sun was shining on the white surface of the lake, making it sparkle with a million pinpricks of light. A strong breeze blew from the east, cooling the horses and keeping us reasonably comfortable in our travelling clothes.

Later in the morning, the road surface became sandy and slowed the horses down. When we came to even deeper sand, we all had to get out and walk – except Mr Snell, of course.

Just on dusk, we stopped at Hunt's Dam to camp for the night. I was tired, stiff and uncomfortable. Fortunately we were the only party camping there and the high bank of the dam gave me enough privacy to relieve myself for the first time that day.

There was a strong smell of camel at the dam. Flies crawled all over us, but we managed to fill several water bags with drinkable water. Mr Snell suggested we spend the night half a mile further on to avoid the worst of the flies and the smell. He moved the coach upwind and unhitched the horses. He fed them some hay and put hobbles on their front legs while we scoured the area for brush and sticks to light a fire. Mr Snell made damper and put water in the billy to boil. It was almost dark by the time we had eaten.

I got out my bed-roll. The men kindly rigged a tarpaulin over the coach, covering its windows. I thanked them and climbed inside to lie down full-length on the floor. It had been a long and tiring day, but I could not sleep at first. My family, Jack, the Finnertys, Mary and the new baby due any day now, all the events of the last few months kept circling around in my mind.

I had never been apart from my whole family before, and I wondered how I would cope without them, but I was surprised to find that I was sad to leave Mrs Finnerty, who had become like an older sister to me. She was about thirty, the same age as Mary, but she and the warden had only been married for six months. As I did the cleaning she would tell me about her travels in England and India, where she met Mr Finnerty. I was hoping to travel to places like that myself, one day, after I strike it rich. Mrs Finnerty was always interested in what I thought about things, too. She asked about the places where we had lived and where I had been educated. I told her that mostly there were no schools on new diggings, but Mother had been very strict when it came to lessons. She had a leather-bound copy of the Bible and a very big book of Shakespeare's plays and sonnets. The black-and-white sketches in the *Complete Works of Shakespeare* were dull compared to the beautiful coloured pictures in Mother's Bible. The dramatic scene of Moses parting the Red Sea and the glowing image of a pregnant Mary, sitting side-saddle on a donkey, were my favourites. Although the Virgin Mary didn't look as if she was 'great with child', in spite of what the words said. And I knew that side-saddle was not the best way to ride a horse. It would only have to raise a trot and you would fall off. Each glossy picture was pasted onto a single page and Mother fretted about the edges of these colour plates being damaged.

'Now you must turn the pages carefully,' she told us when we started to read the book for ourselves. By the time Susan had learned to read, the corners of some of the pictures had come loose. Mother made a paste from flour and water and carefully glued them down again. Over the years these books became even more battered than her copy of the *Encyclopaedia of Common Diseases and Remedies.* We were never allowed to read that one. Mother kept it in her special bag with the bandages, scissors and towels, always packed ready for when people needed her help. I was stunned when Mother gave me her precious book.

I can see now that it was a profound vote of confidence in me, and her greatest act of love.

The men were still sitting by the fire, talking in low voices. At first I heard just a blur of sound. Then I began to hear the words they said. Perhaps they thought I was asleep and were speaking a bit louder. Or perhaps I was ready to be distracted from my kaleidoscope of memories. I heard my name and listened more intently.

'You're right. Coolgardie is no place for a growing girl,' Harry was saying.

'I agree,' Will said. 'We should take her back to Southern Cross. She's a nice young lass.'

'Too nice for the likes of us,' they laughed.

Take me back! How dare they? I was a bit sad about leaving, but my journey had only just begun. During the day the heat had been trying, but I had managed to ignore my thirst and only drink when they did. I was aching all over from sitting down for so long and being bounced and jolted over the rough track, but I was not even thinking of giving up. I was tempted to go out and tell them so, but their laughter had died down and everything was quiet.

Then Mac spoke. 'Wind's changed,' he said. 'I can smell them camels again.'

'Mm,' Mr Snell agreed. 'There'll be a big row in Southern Cross when I tell Warden Finnerty about the state of the water here.'

There were sounds of the fire being stoked up for the night and the men settling down in their swags.

⁂

In the morning I heard someone moving around, stirring the embers of the fire into life. The warm bread smell of fresh damper wafted through the air. I sat up, straightened my dress and tidied my hair. As I stepped down from the coach, Mr Snell handed me a pannikin of tea. I set it down on the sand and went around to a sheltered spot behind a small ridge. I gathered up my skirts and squatted there. When I had finished I went back to the camp fire.

'Your tea's here, Clara,' Mr Snell reminded me and pointed to my abandoned pannikin.

I picked it up, but didn't drink from it.

'What's the matter?' Mr Snell asked kindly. 'Why aren't you drinking your tea?'

I hesitated for a moment, but couldn't think of an excuse. So I told him the truth.

'I can't drink it,' I said. 'I heard them talking about the camels fouling the water last night. I wasn't asleep.'

'Oh, that,' Mr Snell gave a short laugh. 'They didn't mean *this* water, did you, boys? Anyway, when it's boiled up it's all right.'

I glanced at the other men. They were nodding.

'It's okay, we're gunna tell Finnerty and Raeside,' Harry said.

'That's right,' Mac agreed. 'And there should be signs on all the waterholes: *Drinking Water Only*. And a couple of tanks out here would help.'

'A bit of rain to fill them would be handy, too,' Harry added.

'I knew a bloke what did a rain dance, once,' Jock said, tipping his head back and draining the last of the tea from his cup.

‘That worked, did it, Jock?’

‘Yeah,’ Jock grinned. ‘Ten years later the town got flooded and he drowned.’

‘All in the timing, eh?’ Mac nodded, straight-faced.

I wondered if their idea about putting up a sign would be any use. Could the Afghan camel drivers read English? And how did the Aborigines feel about their waterholes being fouled? From the stories I had heard in Southern Cross, the native people were shy, but they had been helpful to the first prospectors who came here. Some people said they were becoming more aggressive lately, though. And who could blame them? Most of their water was being used up by thoughtless newcomers and their animals. It didn’t seem fair at all.

*

When the tarpaulin had been folded and the camping gear packed away, we set off again. The road became rougher, stony in some parts, sandy in others. By midday the horses were plodding along in two wheel ruts that stretched out in front and behind us from horizon to horizon amongst the clumps of spinifex.

We travelled for two more days. Each day the sun climbed into a cloudless sky. In the evening we made camp, ate damper and tried to sleep. Dry cold nights turned into dry hot days. We shed our coats and passed the waterbag around, tipping it up and drinking from the spout, then carefully wiping it before passing to the next person. A plume of red dust rose constantly into the air behind us. While we continued heading east, the hot wind blew the dust away, but whenever the track veered north or south, to avoid some pothole or deep sand trap, our own dust blew back on us and into the coach. We tied handkerchiefs over our mouths and noses. They made us look like a band of bushrangers and I smiled at the thought of Moondyne Joe. I longed for the shade of the spindly gum and the distraction of Joe telling his stories.

The horses suffered more than we did. Their steps slowed as each day went on and we camped a little earlier in the evenings to let them rest. Mr Snell gave them hay because, unlike camels, they could not eat the dry, spiky spinifex and we had not seen a blade of grass for a hundred miles.

On this seemingly endless journey I had a lot of time to think. Pa had written to us in Southern Cross. He said that he missed us and talked about coming to join us. We had written back telling him about life in the Cross and how it was not all sand, sin and sorrow, as we had been told. But what would he make of the new diggings? As we bumped along the narrow track, I wondered what I would find there. Perhaps Jack was right. Perhaps I was making a big mistake. Then I thought of all that gold. They said you didn't even have to dig for it. Gold was lying on top of the ground, just waiting to be picked up. I imagined Pa being even more impatient to see it than I was. Bayley's Reward Reef was already the stuff of legend. The biggest find ever made in Australia. Maybe the biggest in the world! I couldn't wait to see it for myself.

# OCTOBER 1892

We had just set off on the fourth day of our journey when I was startled by a group of kangaroos. They stood up from the hollow where they had been sleeping, just a few yards off the track. The largest would have been at least as tall as Mr Snell. The animal stood, calm and still, his red-brown coat blending with the landscape. Only his pointed ears moved, flicking back and forth, as if he was trying to make sense of the new sounds invading his land. I counted six kangaroos in the group. They ranged in size from the big male to a tiny joey. For a few minutes they stared at us with their soft brown eyes. Then, at some signal detected only by them, they all moved off together, loping effortlessly away across the flat red plain.

We moved on slowly through the deserted landscape. The syncopated rhythm of the coach as it swayed and bumped over the uneven surface of the road both lulled and disturbed me. On the first day, the men had kept us entertained by swapping increasingly outrageous stories, but now they were withdrawn and silent. Their bodies slumped against the sides of the coach. Their eyes were closed, their legs stretched out, except when we hit an extra-large bump and they jerked awake. Involuntary curses sometimes escaped their lips before they remembered I was there and apologised profusely. At first I accepted their apologies with a polite nod. But as time went on and boredom set in, a contest developed between the men. They smirked and tried to outdo each other. Mildly at first, under their breath, then a little louder and faster each time until, smiling openly, they swore and apologised at the slightest excuse. At first I found this performance quite funny. Then it became ridiculous.

'Bloody hell, you blokes!' I said, unable to hide my irritation any longer. 'Why don't you have a bet on who can swear the loudest?' A shocked silence followed.

'Sorry, miss,' Mac said.

'And don't keep saying sorry! I've heard men swear before, you know.' I folded my arms across my chest and stared out at the flat, featureless country. The men were very quiet. When I glanced sideways I saw their contrite faces. Then Harry started to sing softly, 'I'll Take You Home Again, Kathleen'. One by one the others joined in. At the beginning of the second verse I added my higher, lighter voice. We sang all the verses and when we stopped there was clapping from the driver's seat up front.

'Bravo,' Mr Snell called. Then Jock started up with 'The Bonnie Banks o' Loch Lomond'.

We sang until our throats became as dry as the dust, but at least it seemed to make the time go faster.

When no-one could sing any more, we all lapsed into our dozing positions again. I thought about Mother and was glad that she hadn't heard me swearing at the men.

'Language defines you before all else,' she had always said to Susan and me. Pa swore, and so did the boys. Why were there different rules for them? Anyway, I could make up my own rules now. I was in charge of my life, whether Mother approved or not. I felt very grown up.

⁂

At last, about midday, we began to see signs of human activity. Small piles of rubble dotted the landscape where prospectors had dug holes. There were a few random pegs left in the ground where claims had been marked and later abandoned. Jock had heard a story about a young man, crazy with thirst and dysentery, who staggered into Mr Wisdom's pub in Coolgardie. He carried a rifle and waved it at the men in the bar.

'"Empty your pockets, you thieving bunch of louses,"' Jock imitated the young man's American accent, croaky as a crow. Some heads turned towards the American, Jock reported, but most of the blokes in the bar ignored him – until he shouldered the rifle and rested his finger on the trigger. That got their attention all right. 'Whoever it was stole my nuggets had better own up or I'll shoot every last one of ya!' the young bloke had shouted.

Jock continued, 'Arthur Williams, who is a champion boxer and not someone to be trifled with, was behind the bar. "Now calm down, mate," Arthur says. "Give me the gun and we'll sort this out in no time." But your man there, he was havin' none of it,' Jock changed his voice again. '"Y'all turn out your pockets!" the gunman says, and makes a crazy sweep of the room with his rifle. A couple of blokes look like they'll oblige, but most of them just laugh. "We know you ain't got no ammo in that shooter, Davey," they shout.

'Well your man, Davey, his eyes are rollin' by now,' Jock goes on with the story. 'Suddenly there's a hell of a bang. Everyone looks up and, sure enough, there's a dirty great hole in the roof! Ya coulda knocked 'em all down with the one feather.'

'Just goes to show, eh?' Mac nodded, straight-faced as usual.

'And what happened to the man with the gun?' I asked.

'He fell on the floor,' Jock tells us. 'Stone dead.'

We stared at Jock and waited for him to go on. 'Dunno whether it was a heart attack or the typhoid what got 'im. When the blokes in the bar got over the shock someone moved the body.' There was another expectant pause. 'A small bag of nuggets fell out of his coat.'

We all laughed – not because it was funny. We knew that our own lives could be just as mercilessly cut short at any moment, but the knowledge of it made us feel very much alive.

*

Mr Snell was the first to see it. A glint of sunlight bouncing off an iron roof. He called out and we all sat up. Voices became animated. The rhythmic clanking of the horses' chains and harness picked up pace. We passed a cluster of deserted tents. The end of our long journey was in sight.

# OCTOBER 1892

By the time Mr Snell halted the horses in the centre of the makeshift town, a crowd of twenty or thirty men had gathered.

I stepped down from the coach and a great cheer rose up from the crowd. I looked around to see what they were cheering about.

'Don't worry,' Mr Snell said, lifting my bag down from the luggage rack and putting it by the side of the road. 'It happens any time a lady comes visiting – especially a young one.'

I smiled a little nervously and thanked him for my bag. The waiting men began to crowd in.

'Stand back now,' Mr Snell shouted. 'Give the young lady some room. And let Mr Wisdom through or you won't be getting your mail.'

Then Mr Wisdom was beside me. He picked up my bag in one hand, the mailbag in the other. 'Welcome to Coolgardie, Clara,' he said.

We crossed the road to the Exchange Hotel. It was built of brushwood and canvas with a corrugated iron roof. A handpainted sign above the door declared its name and purpose. Mr Wisdom pushed the door open with his foot and stood back for me to go inside. The bar was also made of brushwood and stretched most of the way along one wall. Dozens of clean glasses hung in wooden frames, shaped for the purpose and suspended with chains above the bar. A row of stools stood in line, some of them already occupied by patrons. The rest of the room was crowded with tables and chairs.

As we entered, a stout woman in a cap and apron came in through a curtained doorway in the back wall.

'Ah, Mrs Fagan,' Mr Wisdom said. 'This is Clara.'

'Hello there,' Mrs Fagan wiped her hands down each side of her apron, leaving two streaks of flour. ''Tis good to have ya here at last, so it is.' Her black, beady eyes almost disappeared as her round cheeks swelled into a smile that took up most of her face. 'Sit ya down, so. We'll have to be sortin' this mail here or we'll have a riot on our hands, but that won't be takin' long. Then ya can tell me all about yerself.'

After three and a half days on the road, the last thing I wanted to do was sit down again, but I needed to make a good impression. Mr Wisdom might change his mind about keeping me on if he thought I wasn't up to the job.

All three of us sat down at one of the tables and Mr Wisdom emptied the mailbag, spreading the letters and packages, turning them so that the names became visible. The hotel was the only official address in Coolgardie, and Mr Wisdom acted as postmaster as well as licensee. Most of the letters simply had a name, followed by the word Coolgardie, spelled in various ways. But one I picked up was addressed to 'Larry at the Sandgropers', another to 'Mr R. Moline, T'othersiders'.

'Just put those together,' Mr Wisdom said. 'The first person who comes into town will pick up all the mail for the camps.'

'T'othersiders?' I asked.

Mrs Fagan smiled. ''Tis what the boys from here are after callin' them from the eastern colonies.' She gave a nod of her head towards the street where knots of men stood around waiting. 'Sandgropers – they're the locals. The other names speak for themselves … Montana, Royal Ascot, Little Italy ... Ya get used to them, so ya do,' she said reassuringly.

⁂

When we had finished sorting the mail, Mrs Fagan took me to my room. It was next to hers at the back of the hotel. She pointed out the bathroom, then left me to unpack.

'I'll be in the kitchen,' she said.

In the bathroom, there was a large china jug and matching bowl on a wooden stand. I lifted the jug but there was no water in it. A sign on the wall said *WATER ON REQUEST – 2/6 per gallon*. Below the printed words, someone had scrawled, *Wash in champagne – it's cheaper.*

Across the yard, a row of cubicles with brushwood posts and canvas walls perched above a latrine-type trench. I went into one of the cubicles and found a wooden tea chest with a circular hole in the top. The edges had been smoothed with sandpaper, and a roughly shaped lid placed over the hole. Even this, and the strong smell of disinfectant, was no match for the flies. They crawled all over it and had to be constantly brushed away. I lifted the lid and a pungent smell rose up. I felt my stomach clench with disgust. But I simply had to go.

Back in my room I unpacked, and hung my two dresses on the empty coat-hangers swinging on a wire that was stretched tight across one corner of the room and served as a wardrobe. I placed my underwear in the small chest of drawers beside the bed and took my mother's precious book out of my bag. As I hugged it tightly to my chest, a wave of homesickness swept over me. I was hot, tired and suddenly longing for my family. My earlier happiness at having no-one to tell me what to do had completely evaporated. I even found myself wishing that Susan was here. She would talk nonstop and expect me to unpack her things as well as my own, but it was strange to be without her.

It took the clatter of pans, and the inviting smell of bacon coming from the kitchen, to bring back the excitement of being in a brand-new place. I was a working woman now, with a real job, earning my own money in the richest field of gold in the world. I couldn't wait to get a closer look at the legendary reef.

I sat on the bed and gave a little bounce of happiness. The fancy curved rails of the iron frame squeaked in protest. A light blanket and linen bedspread covered the clean mattress. This was such a new town that nothing looked worn or lived in yet, except for some of the people.

⁂

I went to the kitchen where Mrs Fagan was cutting a slab of meat into bite-sized pieces.

'Ah, there ya are, Clara. 'Tis famished ya'll be, I expect. Help yerself to scones and tea.' She indicated the buttered scones and teapot she had set out at the other end of the bench. 'When ya're done, ya can be startin' on those taties there. No rest for the wicked, eh?' she winked.

I thanked her politely, drank my tea and set to work peeling a large mound of potatoes.

# NOVEMBER 1892

I had been working for a month now and, although there could be customers in the bar at any time of the day, around evening we were really busy. Prospectors came in with red dust in their hair, their clothes, their boots and under their fingernails. They were hot and thirsty after a day of digging and scraping at the dry, rocky ground, always believing that there would be gold in the next shovelful – or the next, or the one after that. They walked into town or came on horseback, with friends or on their own, carrying their swags with them, or just in the clothes they stood up in. Arthur Williams had been here from the start and had set up a billiard room next door to the bar. He and Mr Wisdom were run off their feet serving hundreds of men each evening. Mrs Fagan and I were kept busy in the kitchen cooking, serving meals and washing dishes.

As the meals were ready I carried them through to the bar. I quickly learned to balance three plates on my outstretched left arm and hold another in my right hand. As I placed them on the bar, Arthur Williams shouted four names above the din until those men came up to collect and pay for their food.

At first there were loud wolf-whistles, and cries of 'Hello darlin'' and 'What's your name, then?' any time I came into the room. My cheeks were usually flushed from working in the hot kitchen and I hoped they wouldn't think I was blushing.

'Pay them no heed, Clara,' Arthur Williams said the first time this happened, and told the men to behave themselves. I held my head high, smiled at everyone, and said nothing.

One man leaned across to his neighbour and said, 'Now there's a sight for sore eyes.'

'Yeah, how about a kiss and a cuddle, darlin' – later – out the back?' the other man shouted.

'Hah! 'Tis dead in a ditch you'll be if you go spoilin' her before I gets me chance,' another voice called. The men laughed loudly, nudging each other and downing their drinks. I was so tempted to tell them where to get off, but kept my mouth shut and went back to the kitchen.

'Sure 'tis only the drink talkin', Clara,' Mrs Fagan said. 'They don't see many women out here – especially not young ones. Carry a big stick when ya go out the back on yer own, and ya'll do all right, so ya will.'

'Oh, I'm not afraid of them,' I told her. 'I have two older brothers. They taught me to stand up for myself.'

Mrs Fagan looked hard at me, then she smiled. 'That's the spirit,' she said, and deftly ladled meat and gravy onto plates. I added thick slices of the bread we'd baked that morning and loaded the plates onto my arm. As I placed them on the bar I felt a pinch on my bottom. I swung around and slapped the offending prospector's hand – hard. The shocked look on his face told me he wouldn't be trying that again. I looked at Mr Wisdom to see if he was cross, but he was smiling broadly.

'Serves you right, Joe Quigley,' he said, just loudly enough.

⁂

One morning after I had been in Coolgardie for a couple of weeks, I walked out to Fly Flat before I started work for my first glimpse of Bayley's Reward. Although the mine had been set up at one end there was still almost a mile of reef lying there untouched. The sun was just rising above the top of the ridge, lighting up patches of gold embedded in a jutting rock at the other end. The faint glow seemed to come from deep within the rock, enticing me closer and adding an air of mystery to the sleeping giant.

The day would be blazing hot, but I had quickly come to love those early mornings when the light was pale and soft, the air cool and dry and the birds all squabbling, calling to each other and shouting a warning if I came too close. This was the time when the men in the camps were sleeping off the loud activities of the night before, resting ahead of another day of backbreaking work.

⁂

Mr Snell's coach arrived just before midday one Thursday in mid-November, which was earlier than the week before, so the crowd of waiting prospectors was still quite small. I hurried across the road to see if there was a letter for me from Mother or Susan.

'Clara! How are you?' Mr Snell called as he climbed down from his seat behind the horses.

'Fine, thank you, Mr Snell.'

'You are certainly looking well – better than I had expected,' he said, as he pulled out the mailbag from the rack under the coach. 'Mrs Fagan's parcel is here, but no letters for you today, I'm afraid.'

I took the mailbag from him, trying not to feel too disappointed about the letters. 'Have you seen my mother and sisters lately?' I asked.

'Oh, yes. I sometimes see them shopping in the town, but they are all working every hour God sends. The Cross is bursting at the seams with all this gold rush traffic and Tom Farren's hotel is doing well. His missus had a baby boy, so they're on top of the world.'

'Please give them my love, if you're talking to them,' I said, and walked back across the road, promising myself I would write to them as soon as I finished work.

'Ah, at last!' Mrs Fagan exclaimed when I handed her the large parcel wrapped in brown paper. It was firm, but flexible, and I wondered what could be inside. Mrs Fagan quickly loosened the string and slipped it off. The paper began to unfold at one end. 'Just the ticket,' she said, shaking out a length of turkey-red twill and testing it between her finger and thumb. She looked me up and down, her eyes resting on my hips. 'Aye,' she nodded. 'I'm thinkin' we could tweak the pattern to fit ya, right enough.'

It was not until all the mail was sorted and we had

gone back to the kitchen that Mrs Fagan revealed the reason for the length of red material.

'Bloomers,' she said. 'I never can get them white, no matter how much I'm washin' them. So I'm after thinkin' some red ones would do better – match the colour of the water, like.' Her cheeks were rosy and she looked very pleased with her purchase. I had noticed that, when she smiled, she nearly always kept her mouth closed. It was her way of keeping the flies out, without having to flap her hands at them all the time. Her hands were rarely free for such luxuries while she cooked and scrubbed and swept. 'There's material aplenty here, Clara,' she added. 'Enough to make bloomers for ya an' all ... if ya'd like.'

'That is very kind of you, Mrs Fagan,' I said, hiding my own smile as I turned away to carry the kitchen bin out and empty it on the compost heap behind the dunnies.

⁂

Early the next morning, Mrs Fagan was busy in the kitchen, but she wasn't cooking or washing dishes. She had spread the red material out on the table with a paper pattern laid on top. Quickly and confidently she cut around the edges of the paper. When she had finished cutting out two pairs of large bloomers, she handed the remaining twill to me. 'Do ya know how to sew?' she asked.

'Yes, but my stitches are not very neat. My mother is much better at sewing. She usually does mine.'

'Ah, wait we'll see,' Mrs Fagan said. 'When I'm done I can help with yers.'

Mrs Fagan liked the old-fashioned style of bloomers

with the frills around the legs. Two pairs were duly sewn but, before she would wear them, she insisted they must be washed. Washing day was Monday and, after the hotel closed for the night, Mrs Fagan hung her new bloomers out to dry on the piece of wire stretched across the opening of the brush shed out the back.

In the morning I went for my usual walk. As I passed the open shed, I noticed that Mrs Fagan's bloomers were not hanging on the wire clothes line.

'She must have already brought them in,' I thought, although I hadn't heard her moving around yet.

Leaving the town behind me, I walked out to my favourite rocky outcrop. It rose only a few feet from the surface of the plain and the largest rock had a scooped-out shape to it, almost like a low chair. I sat in it, leaning back and filling my lungs with the cool, fresh air. I lifted my arms to feel the gentle breeze all the way down my body. Far out on the horizon, the distant hills of the breakaway country interrupted the flat line between earth and sky. A few spindly gum trees caught the breeze, their clumps of leaves swaying thirty feet above some dusty tents that were almost invisible in the red-brown landscape. With all this empty space around me, I felt like the only living, breathing thing in the world, but I wasn't lonely. Mrs Fagan and Mr Wisdom were very kind. Arthur Williams often brought me cold drinks in the middle of the day and I was getting to know some of the other men. A great sense of freedom filled me and I smiled to myself.

The sun rose above the plain. Pale shadows slanted across the sand and I knew it was time to make my way back to town. I began to skip, then run, lifting my skirts and thrusting my chin high to celebrate the morning. A startled family of kangaroos scrambled to their feet, stared at me, then loped away. The two smaller ones stopped briefly, looked back, then scampered off to catch up with their parents.

The track took me past a stand of kurrajongs, their trunks now glowing pink and purple as the sun rose higher. In the distance I could see the straight strip of road going up the ridge to where the coach had stopped and we had looked down on the roof of the hotel for the first time. How long ago was that? It seemed like a lifetime since I arrived, slightly nervous, but determined to make a good impression. I thought back and counted on my fingers. Just over a month had passed. Coolgardie had been officially declared a town. Every day brought new people, new challenges and a sense that the known world was behind me, a new one almost within my reach. Was this the same feeling that drove the early explorers so deep into this country, in spite of the hardships, and the dangers they faced?

I noticed how high the sun had risen and quickened my pace.

As I came closer to the town I could hear a lot of voices shouting and laughing. Clusters of men had gathered in the main street. They were all looking in the same direction, some bending double with laughter, others slapping their knees and pointing. Then I saw what they were looking at.

# NOVEMBER 1892

I squeezed my eyes shut then popped them open. I saw a donkey, large as life, staggering along the street. It had a pair of red bloomers pulled up over its back legs. Another pair was tied upside down on its head, like a bonnet, with one ear sticking out of each frilled leg-hole.

Just then Mrs Fagan came storming out of the hotel. She was waving a broom and shouting, 'Which one of yeh thievin' no-hopers has made off with me bloomers? Own up right now or I'll be takin' this broom to the lot o' ya!'

When she saw the donkey, she stopped mid-stride. Her mouth fell open and she started to splutter as if, at that moment, she didn't know whether to laugh or cry.

The men scattered into doorways and around corners. The street was suddenly deserted, except for the donkey. It was bucking and braying at the top of its voice, turning in circles and not proving to be a good advertisement for the comfort of red bloomers. Finally two brave souls ran out and tried to catch it. They struggled, between fits of laughter, but managed to catch hold of the animal's tail. It tried to bite them and they had to dodge its flying hooves while they tugged the splitting bloomers off its legs.

At this point I saw the accordion player, Padraig Murphy from the Tipperary camp, come out from Tobias's Store to lend a hand. He grabbed the donkey's head and untied the bloomers from around its ears. To show off this achievement, Padraig turned to his cheering audience and waved the bloomers in the air. The donkey saw its chance and butted him in the back. The bloomers flew out of Padraig's hand, lifted up with the wind, then fluttered down to drape themselves over his hat. More cheers and shouts of laughter came from the men who had come out of hiding to get a better view of the action.

'There ya go, missus,' Padraig said, plucking Mrs Fagan's bloomers off his hat and handing them to her with a bow. The donkey skittered away as fast as it could go and I couldn't help laughing with the crowd. But Mrs Fagan was not amused. She banned all three men from the bar for a week, in spite of their protests.

'Aw, come on, missus. We did you a favour!'

'Ya did me no favour, ya scalpeen! Stealin' me underwear from me very own backyard!' Mrs Fagan declared.

'Not me!' Padraig protested. 'I didn't steal 'em.'

'Nor me!' the others chorused. 'Fair's fair …'

They might as well have saved their breath. By then Mrs Fagan had crossed the road, swung open the door of the hotel and trounced back inside, clutching both pairs of red bloomers and shaking her broom.

*

I went to my room, put on my apron, brushed my hair and wound it tightly around my head, tucking it in and pinning the ends. Then I wiped the red dust off my boots and joined Mrs Fagan in the kitchen.

'Teapot's still warm,' she said, glancing in my direction, before turning her attention back to dividing and shaping the leavened bread dough, which had stood on the hob of the wood stove overnight and risen to twice its original size. The remains of yesterday's loaf were set out on the table. I cut a slice, speared it on the wire prongs of the toasting fork and blew a fine layer of ash from the coals in the grate. They glowed, red and inviting, as I held the bread over them on the long-handled fork. The warm smell of toast filled the room.

'Are your bloomers damaged beyond repair, Mrs Fagan?' I asked, sitting down to eat my toast and drink my tea.

'Aeh, lass, t'was just a prank,' Mrs Fagan said. 'There's little enough entertainment for the boys out here, and no real harm done. That's not to say ya can let 'em think they got away with it, mind. Ya must show 'em who's boss.' She carried the tray of uncooked loaves to the large brick oven and slid them in.

*

Drinking water was in such short supply that everyone looked forward to the arrival of Jack and his team of horses bringing the precious liquid from the dams and wells his father owned. When the anxiously awaited column of dust appeared on the horizon on a Saturday the men gathered with their billies, pans and converted kerosene tins with handles.

I also watched eagerly for that telltale dust. For me it meant that Jack would soon be here. Since he started coming regularly there were always things I wanted to tell him and he would bring me news of my family and gossip from the Cross.

When he arrived for his third run in late November, I went to the door of the hotel and waved to him as his team pulled up outside. He called back to me from his seat behind the horses while eager men crowded around with pouches of gold or money in their hands. They were all clamouring to be served first, just in case the water ran out.

It would be a busy day for us because most of the men who had made the trip into town to collect their water would stay on, drinking in the bar, playing billiards and sometimes renting rooms for the night. On days like this I flew through the extra work, thinking about Jack and looking forward to sharing all the things I had been saving up to tell him.

# NOVEMBER 1892

When the meals had all been served, the dishes washed and the dough prepared for tomorrow's bread, I stepped out onto the verandah. Jack was there, leaning against the post.

'Well, my lady, where shall we go tonight?' he said. 'Theatre? Cabaret? Restaurant?'

I tilted my head to one side and pretended to weigh up these suggestions. Then I said, 'I'm a little tired tonight, sir. Let's go for a stroll.'

'As you wish,' he said, making an exaggerated bow and holding out his hand to me as if I was Cinderella going to the ball with the handsome prince. Not that Jack was handsome – well not in the tall and dark way that you read about in books of fairytales. He had an open, friendly face with lively blue eyes and thick brown hair that always seemed to need brushing off his forehead. He was fun to be with. He made me laugh, but he could be serious, too. I knew that I could talk to him about anything. Sometimes we had heated arguments, but we were still friends afterwards. Lots of men in Coolgardie wanted to be my friend, and I was happy to be theirs. I danced with them at the pub when the Irishmen came to town to play their squeezeboxes and tin whistles, or the Americans with their banjos. We had a grand time singing and laughing together. But I knew those men only saw me on the outside. When Jack looked at me with his eyes half closed I felt he could see who I really was – on the inside.

While Jack was in town we went for long walks and talked nonstop. I told him about the red bloomers, which he thought was hilarious. I asked about my family and friends back in the Cross. He told me the new baby was giving Mary and Tom a hard time, but his sisters adored him and spoiled him rotten.

Emily had sent me a catalogue. She knew there were no dress shops in Coolgardie, and it took more than a month for anything to come from Perth, but she told Jack that I should at least look at the latest fashions. Susan wanted to know when I was coming back for a visit. And there was a water supply dispute going on in the town. Jack had seen Mother and Tom at the Town Council meeting where Warden Finnerty was speaking about the problem of camels and horses fouling the waterholes between Southern Cross and Coolgardie. There were still several hundred prospectors using the track each week, he told the meeting, and more lives would be lost if the water wasn't kept clean.

I asked Jack about the dances in the Cross, too. We compared them with the ones here in Coolgardie, which were rarely organised in advance but tended to happen spontaneously.

'I saw Padraig in town earlier today,' I said to Jack. 'He might have the music going by now.'

'Should we go and see?' Jack asked.

'Of course,' I told him. 'Why not?'

'I thought you might like to be alone with me,' he teased and moved closer. I bumped him away with my shoulder – but gently.

⁂

Jack stayed for two more nights to rest his horses. When my work was done each day we would walk out of town for several miles, often in the direction of the chair-shaped rocky outcrop.

It was well after ten o'clock on the second night and the easterly wind was blowing. The air had cooled but the rock was still warm. I sat down and Jack sat beside me. He ran his hand idly over the bulge of the rock and said, 'I wonder if we are sitting on a gold mine.'

I stood up and examined the rock. On my morning walks I had often seen the tiny flecks of feldspar glinting on its surface as the sun came up. I knew that feldspar was only fool's gold. It shone like gold, but was absolutely worthless, so I hadn't taken much notice.

'Do you really think there could be gold in this rock?' I asked.

'No,' Jack said. 'Just wishful thinking.'

'I thought you weren't interested in gold.'

'I didn't say that,' Jack protested. 'It's just frustrating, knowing it's there, but not being able to find it.'

'But that's no reason to give up,' I said. 'Real prospectors never give up.'

'Neither do the chancers, the con men, the criminals escaping from the law. They cluster around goldfields like bloodsucking leeches.'

'Maybe they're looking for a new start, a place where nobody knows them?' I said.

'Like Moondyne Joe, you mean?'

'Yes, a bit like that. Anyway, Pa isn't one of those. Some prospectors just can't resist the pull of gold. Even after they've struck it rich, they keep going back out there. Pa is like that, always searching. He's never really struck it rich, but he never gave up. Not until Susan was born.

'Mother had a very hard time with her. She could barely leave her bed for three months, and even then it was all she could do to take care of the baby. Mary and Emily looked after us and Billy and Joe went prospecting with Pa. Pa decided we couldn't keep moving on forever. He got a job, working for wages at Cooper's Mine, but he never threw away his panning dish or his rock pick. I could tell that, as soon as we were old enough to care for ourselves, he would go off prospecting again.'

Jack was looking thoughtful. 'Some people call it gold fever,' he said at last.

'Mother does,' I grinned. 'Sometimes I think I caught that fever from Pa. It's just so exciting to think about gold lying in the ground, like buried treasure, waiting to be discovered. Don't you think?'

At first, he didn't answer. He brushed the hair off his forehead and I noticed the deeper furrows. 'It's a mug's game,' he said. 'Although …' He held out his hand to me and I pulled him up off the rock. 'Our dams and soaks have almost dried up. More condensers are being built to purify the bore water as it fills up the shafts.'

'Did you hear that Martin Walsh had a stroke of luck the other day?' I asked.

Jack shook his head. 'Is he the bloke drilling for the government?'

'Yes. He put down a bore just off Bayley Street and struck water! It's not much more than a trickle,' I said. 'And brackish. We can't drink it, but it's good for the washing.'

Jack looked thoughtful. 'There may come a time …'

We walked slowly back towards the town, thinking our own thoughts. As we came closer, we heard music.

'Come on,' Jack said and quickened his pace. 'Sounds like a singalong.'

# NOVEMBER 1892

The new Miner's Institute was packed with people. Twice as many as we used to fit into the dining room at the hotel. A banjo and a tambourine had joined Padraig's accordion and his friend Liam's tin whistle. The dance was in full swing.

Jack held my hand and forged a path for us through the crowd, greeting people as we went. Between us we knew most of the people in the hall.

During a break in the dancing, I went up to say hello to Padraig. He was sitting on his own in the band's rest area, his accordion on his lap. At first, he didn't notice me as he bent over the instrument, concentrating on some adjustment he was making to the strap. When he did look up, his face was drawn and serious.

'Are you all right, Padraig?' I asked. He gave me a half smile and a nod, but I wasn't convinced.

'Sure, I'm fine,' he mumbled, head down again. 'But Donal is in a real bad way.'

'Why? What happened?' I asked, leaning closer.

'Silly bugger,' Padraig said. 'Got himself into a fight over some claim or other.'

'So?' I prompted. A fight over a claim was hardly unusual in the crowded camps.

'So, one man's dead already. And Donal ...' Padraig lifted his eyes to mine, but seemed to have run out of words. Liam came back to his seat and began to clean his tin whistle. 'Donal took a bullet in his chest.' Padraig spoke just loud enough for me to hear. 'It obviously missed his heart. He's alive, but strugglin' to breathe.'

'Where is he?' I asked.

'Out at Tipperary. I didn't want to leave him there on his own, but he told me to bugger off.'

'I could come out in the morning,' I said tentatively, 'to see if there is anything I can do.'

Padraig looked surprised. 'Are ya a doctor?' he asked. The only doctor in the town had already left to go back to the city.

'No, but I have my mother's medical book. If he survives the night, I might be able to help.' Perhaps it was foolish of me to offer, but I didn't like to see Padraig so upset. Many times I had gone with Mother to help her attend to sick people, but never on my own. Still, Padraig was my friend and I wanted to help if I could.

When I told Jack, he was horrified, but I had promised Padraig.

'I can see that you are determined to do this, Clara, but at least let me come with you,' he said eventually.

*

In the morning Jack was at my door at first light. We walked out to Tipperary, where the tents were roughly grouped together with washing lines strung between them. Picks, shovels, panning dishes, empty kerosene tins, pots and pans and all manner of things were strewn around in heaps and bundles.

'How do they know which tools are theirs?' I asked Jack.

'They don't,' he said. 'They just share them all.'

Padraig saw us coming and came out to meet us. In a bag on my shoulder I carried my mother's book, some clean towels, and bandages I'd made by boiling up some of the cleaning rags. I had looked up the treatment for bullet wounds in Mother's book the night before, and it seemed there was little I could do without surgery. Padraig offered to take the bag but I said I needed to keep it with me.

'I'll need hot water,' I said.

'Sure I'll give the fire a poke, so,' Padraig said, indicating the small circle of rocks with glowing coals in the middle. A tripod had been erected over it and an iron pot suspended from a hook at the top.

'Where's your friend?' I asked as Padraig went to stoke the remains of last night's fire. He pointed to a faded tent.

Jack and I made our way past a decaying pile of rubbish and the stinking latrine trench that served the whole camp. I covered my mouth and nose and raised my eyebrows at Jack.

'How can they live like this?' I muttered.

'What?' he said. I shook my head. He lifted the tent flap and a cloud of flies rose into the air. The stench from inside was almost as bad as the one from the latrines.

The sound of Donal's tortured breathing was the first thing I heard. He lay on a camp bed, a grubby army blanket covering his legs and a blood-soaked shirt discarded on the ground beside him. Blood had congealed around a wound just below his right collarbone. Flies crawled around the open wound and I brushed them away. Donal's eyes remained closed. His chest heaved as he sucked at the air.

I looked around the inside of the tent. There was another camp bed and a wooden box full of who knows what, but nothing else in the dingy space.

Padraig came back from stoking the fire and I asked him if there was a chair in the camp at all.

'I need something to sit him up in,' I explained. Jack was dispatched to one of the other tents where, hopefully, he would find a folding chair.

Padraig bent over his friend. 'Donal, can ya hear me, mate?' Donal opened his eyes, but it was obvious that the act of breathing was taking every ounce of concentration he could muster. 'This is Clara. She's going to help ya.' I thought I saw a slight nod of Donal's head before his eyes closed again.

Jack returned with a deckchair. He unfolded it and set it beside the bed. The striped canvas seat flopped down in the wooden frame, making a kind of cradle. Padraig stood behind Donal's head and slid his hands under his friend's armpits. A low animal groan came from the injured man's open mouth. I saw that the thin mattress cover, which was also soaked in blood, had stuck to Donal's skin. It tore away as his shoulders were raised, exposing a matching hole in his back. The bullet had gone right through his shoulder.

‘Wait,’ I said, and moved closer to examine this second wound. It looked cleaner than the other one and I was hoping that there were no fragments of the bullet left inside to complicate things. I gave him a nod and Jack lifted Donal’s legs. Between them, Jack and Padraig transferred the man’s tense body into the chair. Fitful moans escaped from his mouth between each gasping breath. I needed him to sit more upright in the chair, to help his breathing, so Padraig brought the grubby pillows from both beds. Jack lifted Donal while Padraig stuffed the pillows under him. He gave a sharp cry of pain and bright blood oozed from his wound. I tried to stay calm.

‘Is that water hot yet?’ I asked Padraig, who immediately went out. He came back with a steaming kerosene tin full of water. I took a face cloth out of my bag, dipped a corner of it in the water and, as gently as I could, wiped away blood and maggots from the wound. Then I placed a wad of towel over it, lifted Donal’s hand and pressed it against the towel.

‘Hold this in place,’ I told him. He looked at me with despairing eyes. I wrapped a smaller towel around the kerosene tin and held it under his nose.

‘Breathe in the steam,’ I said, but there was very little steam left. Even so, his breathing seemed easier, now that he was in a more upright position.

‘Do you have any rum or brandy?’ I asked Padraig.

‘We gave it to him already,’ he said.

‘Did it help?’ I asked.

‘It did,’ Donal said. We looked at him in surprise. His voice was hoarse and strained, but at least he had spoken. I smiled and wished him well. Then I picked up my bag and stepped outside. It was such a relief to be out in the fresh air that I opened my mouth to suck it in, and a fly flew straight in. I gagged and spat it out. Padraig and Jack followed me out of the tent.

'Come into town and get some brandy,' I told Padraig.

'That would brighten me day, so it would,' he said.

'For him! Not for you.'

'Sure, I'm only jokin',' he laughed. 'Old Donal is lookin' so good now, I'll not be surprised if he's back at the dance next week.'

I was wishing I felt as confident as Padraig sounded – or was he just trying to make me feel better? I had done all I could, but it wasn't much.

'We'll have to wait and see,' I said. As soon as I'd spoken I could hear Mother's voice in my head saying exactly the same thing. I cleared my throat and went on. 'Make sure you keep that wound of his clean. And if you hear him wheezing bring boiling water and a towel. Put the towel over his head and get him to breathe in the steam. If the bullet hasn't punctured his lung he might survive. I think Mrs Fagan has some powders he could take for the pain.'

'I'm indebted to ya, Clara, so I am,' Padraig said, sounding serious again.

'No bother,' I said. 'I hope he recovers.'

Jack and I waved to Padraig as he disappeared into the tent.

# DECEMBER 1892

When Mrs Fagan told Mr Wisdom that it was almost impossible for me to finish my work, he agreed to employ more help. In the two months since Coolgardie had been declared a town it had grown to four times its original size. Six condensers worked away at purifying the underground water. Although it was still not safe to drink and had to be boiled and cooled, at least we could use it for washing and cleaning. Bayley's Mine at Fly Flat employed almost a hundred men. Some of them had even brought their wives and children. Transport companies delivered stores, timber and building materials. Real houses, built from weatherboard and corrugated iron, were springing up, and Tobias's Store had expanded. A large shed had been built at the back to hold extra stock.

Even on my morning walk I could feel the heat of summer approaching, but my spirits lifted when Mrs Fagan greeted me with the news that Warden and Mrs Finnerty were coming to live in Coolgardie.

'They'll be stayin' here with us, so they will, until their own place is built,' she said. She was smiling so much that her round cheeks almost hid her deep-set black eyes.

'Oh, Mrs Fagan, that's wonderful news!' I said, clapping my hands.

'So it is,' she agreed. 'Mrs Finnerty is a woman of quality. Sure the town will be the better for havin' her here. And the warden, of course.' She looked almost as delighted as I was. There would be even more work, but I didn't care. I would manage, no matter how long it took. Anyway, I was still hoping Mr Wisdom would find someone to come and work here.

⁂

Later that day a willy-willy came down Bayley Street. It started out on the plain. I could see it coming from twenty miles away, swirling the loose particles of sand and dried-out stalks of spinifex into a thin, red-brown column of dust that reached high up into the sky. It swayed and twisted like a demented dancer and I crossed my fingers behind my back. Willy-willies were unpredictable things. Although it seemed to be heading towards us, there were moments when it wavered along its chosen path and I fervently hoped it would veer away and miss the town. I had just finished cleaning all the rooms. A willy-willy would cover them in red dust and grit in less than a minute. I had been late starting that morning. Jack was leaving and I had gone to the stables at first light to say goodbye to him. I knew Mrs Fagan needed me in the kitchen so I hurried through the last of the sweeping, still hoping that the storm might miss us, but my heart sank when I glanced out into the street. The willy-willy was almost upon us.

I ran to the front windows and slammed them shut. Arthur Williams was already rolling down the canvas flaps in the billiard room and tying them tight. Mr Wisdom threw covers over tables in the dining room and tipped chairs upside down, shouting at me to come and help. The willy-willy, which had been silent at a distance, began to hiss and squeal. It came shrieking in under the rafters, lifted a loose corner of the tin roof and slapped it down with a bang. The whole makeshift building shuddered and seemed to lean away from the wind, but there was no keeping it out. It brought the red dust swirling in through every crack.

All four of us huddled together behind the bar, which was the sturdiest part of the building. Mrs Fagan crouched down and pulled the bottom of her apron up over her head. Mr Wisdom and Arthur Williams sat on the floor with their knees drawn up and their hands over their ears. The glasses rattled above us in their wooden racks. I didn't know what to do. There had been dust storms before, but nothing like this. Even in the shelter of the bar, the wind blew my hair about my face and dust into my eyes.

There was a huge clap of thunder overhead. Above the roar of the wind I heard horses screaming and stamping in the stables. Where was Jack? Was he still out there in the storm? I leapt up to go and look for him, but Mrs Fagan caught my arm and pulled me down again.

'Don't be daft, lass,' she yelled in my ear. 'Ya can't be goin' anywhere in this!'

The rain came right behind the willy-willy. When the first fat drops fell, we all stood up and rushed to the door. Rain was splashing onto the dirt, each drop leaving its own tiny moon crater. The dry earth welcomed the moisture and gave off a distinctive smell of wet soil – it made me want to run outside and stand in the rain, to breathe in the freshness of it and feel the cooling drops on my gritty skin.

The rain was now pouring down in sheets. The splashing sound had changed to a steady drumming. Mrs Fagan and I went out into the street. It seemed that the whole town was out there, all in their work clothes, getting soaking wet. The men pulled off their hats and let the rain wash through their hair. The women took off their boots, lifted their skirts and bathed their bare feet. Two children ran splashing through puddles. A toddler who had clearly never seen rain before clung uncertainly to his mother. Mrs Fagan and I looked at each other and laughed at our bedraggled state. Water streamed through our hair and left red stains on our white blouses, which quickly turned to pink as the deluge soaked into our clothes. I lifted my arms to sweep the hair from my eyes. Water trickled down my neck and into my armpits.

The storm was over as quickly as it had begun. Red-brown water coursed down the street, making gullies in the wheel tracks and puddles in the doorways.

The sun came out. People hung their wet clothes over railings, and pegged them onto clothes lines. Neighbours called to each other as they opened their windows.

'Nice drop,' they said.

'Smell that clean air.'

'Any damage?'

'Nothing major over here. How about you?'

Jack came up from the stables. He was soaked to the skin but grinning broadly.

'You okay?' he asked.

'Of course,' I said. 'Isn't it wonderful? Now we can wash everything! And your wells and soaks will be full.'

'Hmm, we'll see,' Jack said, and his face straightened out. 'Storms like this can be very local. It was a big one, but out here they can come through in a strip that's only a mile wide. Lots of places miss out.'

'Oh,' I said, deflated.

'Hey, don't be glum,' Jack's smile returned. 'The track will be too wet for me to go back to the Cross now. I'll be here for another night at least.'

That definitely brightened up my day.

# DECEMBER 1892

A week later, Mr Wisdom told me that Padraig was in the bar and was asking for me. I had been wondering about his friend, Donal, but had been absolutely run off my feet with cleaning up after the willy-willy and helping Mrs Fagan get ready for the Finnertys. I set the lid on the bubbling stew I had been tending and turned to Mrs Fagan.

'Away with ya, lass. I'll finish up here,' she said.

I took off my apron and went through to the bar.

Padraig stood there awkwardly with a wooden vase in his hand. I could see that it had been carved from a gum tree branch. It was beautifully smooth with a polished sheen to the curved surface. The inside had been hollowed out and sealed with varnish to hold water.

'It ain't much,' Padraig said, handing me the vase. 'But I wanted to thank ya for what ya did for Donal.'

'Padraig, it's lovely!' I said, taking his offering and turning it in my hand. Pa sometimes gave bunches of flowers to Mother, but flowers were rare here. 'It will be perfect for the eucalyptus sprigs.' We often cut fresh leaves from the bush and put them in the bedrooms to make them smell nice. 'And how is Donal?' I asked.

'He passed away,' Padraig said, bowing his head and making a sign of the cross.

'Oh.' I looked at the floor. Although I had not really known Donal, my eyes began to rim with tears.

'No, Clara,' Padraig said urgently. 'Don't be upsettin' yerself. I came to thank ya for easin' his pain. He was comfortable, even jolly, in his last few days and he passed peaceful-like, in the night. Father O'Brien said the words and we buried him today.'

'I am so sorry, Padraig,' I said. A longing for my mother threatened to swamp me. If only she had been here, perhaps we could have saved him.

⁂

It was not long before Mother's *Encyclopaedia of Common Diseases and Remedies* had to be put to use again. Word had spread quickly. I made it clear that I had no training, but we were once again without a doctor so that didn't seem to matter.

'Ya've a level head on ya, and a kind heart,' Padraig had reassured me when I commented on this to him at the dance. 'Besides, ya can read what it says in that magic book there.'

'Padraig!' I protested. 'I'm not a witchdoctor! There is nothing magic about it.' But I could see that people were desperate. Even when I knew I could only dispense a little comfort, I could not refuse them.

*

Warden and Mrs Finnerty finally arrived two weeks before Christmas.

The grapevine had been active again and we knew when to expect them. I rushed out to meet the coach.

'Clara! How good to see you.' Mrs Finnerty hugged me and I shook hands with the warden. 'My, you are looking well.'

I laughed and smoothed down my apron, thinking I must look a sight and that she was just being kind, but the warden was nodding. 'Yes, and even more grown up,' he said.

'Oh, John, of course she has grown up. It's been months since we saw you, hasn't it, Clara?'

'Yes, Mrs Finnerty,' I said. 'But I will look after you – just like before. You are to have the brand-new suite and all the best linen and there's water standing ready in the jug for you …' They smiled at each other while I prattled on, and laughed when I finally stopped for breath. I felt myself blushing with the pleasure of seeing them. 'I do hope you will like it here,' I said.

I might have changed, but the Finnertys hadn't. They still felt like family. I had missed them almost as much as I missed Mother and Susan, and had sent a letter back to them in Southern Cross when Jack went last. That was at the end of November but I hadn't heard from them. And I hadn't seen Jack for nearly a month.

Then one day I looked out and saw his team and wagon in the street. I rushed out with my dust cloth still in my hand. Jack looked up and waved, but he was busy exchanging paperwork with someone from Bayley's Mine.

His wagon was loaded with a large engine: a replacement for one of the condensers that had broken down. I went back inside to finish my jobs for the day, knowing that I would see him later once he was done with his work.

⁂

In the evening we strolled out of town and sat down to rest on our usual rocky seat.

'I've been thinking,' Jack said.

I was about to say, 'Did it hurt?', which had become a standard joke between us, but he looked so serious I stopped myself just in time. 'There is so much pressure on our wells and soaks that we don't have much water left to sell out here. And with all those condensers pumping water at the mine, my deliveries are not so vital anymore. Besides, I'm ready for a change. I've saved up some money from my wages. I think I'll try my luck at prospecting after all. See how it goes. What do you think?'

'Are you trying to cramp my style, Jack Raeside?' I said, even though the biggest smile was stretching across my face.

'Heaven help anyone who tries to come between you and what you have decided to do,' he said, giving me his usual cheeky grin. 'No, you can keep your troupe of admirers, as long as they don't expect sympathy from me when you dump them.'

'What, dump them for you?' I huffed.

'Well it's either me or the donkey wearing the red bloomers. No-one else will ever make you laugh as much.'

'Or cry as much.' I giggled at the memory of tears streaming down my face from laughing so much the day the poor old donkey wore Mrs Fagan's red bloomers.

‘That’s settled then,’ Jack said. ‘First dance is mine.’ He stood up and pulled me to my feet. Then, with his arm around my waist, we began to waltz. We stirred up the red dust, scattered some stones and scared a frill-necked lizard. I became helpless with laughter in no time.

That night after I got home I thought a lot about Jack moving to Coolgardie.

*

When Jack and I met again after work the next day, I said, ‘I know what it’s like to dream of striking it rich. But I’ve come to realise that Coolgardie is not like Queensland. Most of these men find so little gold you wonder how they keep going. I never thought I would say this, but I think it might be better to run a hotel. Gold comes and goes, but men will always need a drink.’

‘Or two,’ Jack said.

‘And food.’

‘And a place to sleep, at first.’ We were finishing each other’s sentences, as we used to do.

‘Are you reading my mind again?’ I asked. A small thrill of recognition travelled up my spine. It was as if we had never been apart.

‘I wouldn’t dare,’ Jack smiled, but he wasn’t looking at me. ‘There’s just one problem with your pub idea, though …’ he said thoughtfully. ‘Money.’

*

Jack arranged for fresh horses and set off for the Cross the next day. I waved to him and stood watching while the column of dust from his wagon rose into the still air. I thought about Jack coming to live here. I would be so happy if he did, but I wondered if he would come to regret it. Wispy clouds feathered out across a pale sky and thunder rumbled threateningly in the distance.

# JANUARY 1893

It was a hot day. I was taking my time to wipe down the tables in the dining room, with the damp cloth cooling my hands, when I saw a strange woman walking by along the street. She was dressed in a beautiful flowing gown, gossamer-light, with swirling panels of orange and blue. The fabric was so fine that I could almost see through it and the woman's bare shoulders swayed as she walked. I expected her to come into the hotel, but she went straight past. She must have arrived on Snell's coach, but where could she possibly be going, dressed like that, at this time of day?

I finished setting up the tables and was cleaning the bar when the same woman walked past again, this time in the opposite direction. I hurried through my chores and went out into the yard. Mrs Fagan was hanging out the bedsheets.

'Did you see that woman in the beautiful dress?' I asked her. She nodded. 'Who is she?'

'I couldn't be tellin' ya her name, lass,' Mrs Fagan

replied, removing the pegs she had been holding in her mouth. 'But she's advertisin' her business for all to see.'

'What business is that?' I asked.

'She's a woman of ill fame. Not the first of her kind to arrive here, but the most brazen,' Mrs Fagan told me.

I frowned. 'Is that like a woman of the night?' I asked. 'Pa has told me to stay clear of them.'

'Your Pa is tellin' ya right, Clara, but these women are necessary out here. Women like her could be after savin' decent folks like us from some ... unpleasantness with the men.' I must have looked puzzled because she went on. 'Now that the town is changin', there are many more strangers around.'

I thought about this and wondered if Pa would agree. I wanted to ask Jack what he thought, but he'd gone back to Southern Cross.

The Finnertys' suite was next on my list of jobs for the day. When I knocked on the door, Mrs Finnerty called, 'Come in, Clara.'

I began with the dusting, as I always did, but couldn't resist asking Mrs Finnerty if she had seen the brightly dressed woman.

'I have indeed,' Mrs Finnerty said and frowned. 'She is a notorious prostitute who was working in Southern Cross. She has been the cause of many disputes that the warden has had to deal with.'

'What sort of disputes?' I asked. Mother had never mentioned this woman in her letters, but then I don't suppose she wanted to tell me.

'Mostly over money,' Mrs Finnerty said. 'She charges for her services, which the men expect, but they don't expect to find that their pockets have been emptied as well. Some say she gets them drunk and they fall asleep. Others say she picks their pockets before they have even taken their trousers off.'

'Mrs Fagan says we need women like her here,' I said.

'Does she now?' Mrs Finnerty looked surprised. 'And why is that?'

'She says that women of her kind may well save us from unwanted advances from the men,' I said.

Mrs Finnerty looked thoughtful. 'Perhaps,' she said. 'Although I'm afraid the warden wouldn't agree. He has enough to do sorting out drunken brawls and fights over claims, without unscrupulous women making more trouble. He has been out at the camps all day investigating another suspicious death.'

My hand came up to cover my mouth. 'I hope it's not someone we know,' I said.

'He didn't say,' Mrs Finnerty replied. 'But the doctor has recorded cyanide poisoning as the cause of death.' A doctor had arrived with the latest influx of prospectors. He had left his practice in the city to try his luck, but was constantly being called on to deal with medical problems and didn't have much time for prospecting. 'Cyanide is commonly called the woman's weapon, you know,' she added.

'She only arrived this morning,' I protested. 'And surely such a beautiful woman would not murder anyone!' I stood there with the feather duster dangling from my hand. Mrs Finnerty took me by the shoulders.

'Ah, Clara, you are such a trusting soul,' she said. 'A woman may be as beautiful as the sun, but have a heart of soot.'

*

Mr Wisdom was once again finding it near impossible to get staff to come out as far as Coolgardie to work, in spite of the higher wages he was offering. He had almost given up when a young woman from England replied. A month after he had first advertised the position, a stranger climbed nimbly down from Mr Snell's coach. She was small and dainty, but sensibly dressed, and I liked her immediately.

'Hello, you must be Florrie,' I said and shook her hand. 'I'm Clara. Come on in, I'm sure you're exhausted.' Although I did think she looked remarkably fresh and full of life.

'Oh no, I'm too excited to be tired,' Florrie told me. 'Everything is so new and different. I have already learned to build a camp fire and sleep under the stars. And I met a real bushranger in Southern Cross. The new policeman tried to arrest him, but he talked his way out of it.'

'Moondyne Joe,' I laughed. 'He's got a silver tongue on him, that one. You can't believe a word he says, but he tells great stories.'

'I've never met anyone like him,' Florrie said. 'I felt as if I had stepped right into the pages of a Boy's Own adventure book. Then we saw kangaroos and an emu and a whole flock of black cockatoos. So different from England.'

'Have you just come all the way from England?' I asked.

'Not today,' she laughed. 'I arrived in Fremantle four weeks ago.'

'I hope you like it here,' I said, thinking that life in Coolgardie would be quite a shock for her.

'Oh, I'm sure I will,' she said.

'Here you go, miss,' Mr Snell placed Florrie's travel bag down beside her.

'Thank you,' she said. 'You have been very kind.'

I immediately thought of my own arrival in Coolgardie. The town had already changed so much since then, but I still remembered how kind people were.

'Your mother sends her love, Clara, and says she will write soon,' Mr Snell said, before he climbed back up to his seat behind the horses.

⁂

Florrie seemed to settle in over the next few weeks as if she had always been with us. She was quick and confident, always up for a challenge, and we became great friends. I told her about Jack and the dances and parties.

'There don't seem to be many young women around,' she said.

'You'll be very popular,' I grinned. 'I hope you don't mind dancing all night.'

'I love dancing,' Florrie said. 'As long as no-one gets too serious.'

'Oh, they'll all want to marry you,' I laughed.

'Then they will just have to wait in line,' she said. 'And anyone who misbehaves can go to the end of the queue.'

I asked Florrie about England.

'Cold, damp, grey,' she told me.

I was disappointed. 'But what about Buckingham Palace, the Grenadier Guards, the Queen? Isn't it all very grand?'

'Oh yes, but they're in London. I come from Sussex.'

'What's that like?' I asked.

'It's beautiful,' she said. 'Lush grass, white sheep grazing on the hills, but not enough sunshine. I'm bored with all that misty rain on green fields.'

'That's lucky,' I smiled at her. 'We have sunshine. And we're definitely short on green fields.'

Although Mrs Fagan's tongue could be sharp at times, she mothered us both and made it clear to the men in town that anyone who tried to get too physical with her girls would have to deal with her as well.

We both worked hard, but it was fun to have someone younger than Mrs Fagan to talk to. When it came to the dances, we made a pact with each other. We would dance with all the men equally, and not favour just one – when Jack wasn't here, of course. We didn't want them fighting over us.

# APRIL 1893

The weather had continued to be very hot for the whole of March, going on into April. One Saturday afternoon, I was setting up the tables in the dining room when a man staggered in through the main door. He took off his hat and I saw that it was Paddy Hannan. He was a well-known prospector who had been camped out past Tipperary for a while. Although he was never very sociable, like Arthur Bayley, he had a reputation for being able to smell gold. He had left Coolgardie three or four weeks back to try his luck further east. Paddy had never been a big man, but always strong and wiry. Now his face was gaunt, his lips were dry and cracked, his skin seemed to hang loose on his bones and the whites of his eyes had a yellowish tinge to them. He was asking for a room, but I had to tell him that the hotel was absolutely full.

'Would ya not have a corner of the stables, then? I'd be happy to share with me horse.' He spoke slowly, pausing for breath between the words. His body swayed and he put one hand on a table to steady himself. I quickly pulled out a chair.

'Please, sit here,' I said. 'I'll see what I can do.' He sank gratefully onto the chair.

I went to find Mrs Fagan and told her that Paddy was in the dining room. 'I know we are full,' I said, 'but he looks terribly ill. He can have my room – just for a few days – and I'll bunk in with Florrie. I'm sure she won't mind.'

Mrs Fagan looked hard at me. 'Ya've a good heart, Clara, but we can't be takin' in any old prospector who comes along, especially one who is already ill. How do we know he won't be passin' on some dreadful disease to the rest of us?'

'Oh, please, Mrs Fagan. We can't turn him away. What if he dies? I will always blame myself.'

'Aeh, child, these men know what they're comin' to.'

'But sometimes they don't. I meet them at the dances and some of them have been told the most terrible lies. They believe that there is so much gold lying in the streets of Coolgardie that anyone who comes here will pick up a fortune – before lunchtime.'

Mrs Fagan sighed. She went to the open doorway between the kitchen and dining room and looked in. I stood close behind her and peeped over her shoulder.

'Ya're right, Clara,' Mrs Fagan said softly. 'He looks awful peaky, so he does.' He was slumped in the chair with his mouth hanging open, his eyes closed. We need not have worried that he would see us watching him. He looked as if he might never open his eyes again.

Mrs Fagan crossed the room and tapped him gently on the shoulder.

'Mr Hannan,' she said. '"Tis true we've no rooms left, but Clara has offered ya hers.'

He opened his eyes. 'No, no,' he said. 'Very kind … couldn't possibly.' He tried to stand but his legs would not support him and he fell back onto the chair.

'Come, now,' Mrs Fagan said firmly. She was a strong woman and lifted him easily to his feet. Putting her shoulder under one of his arms, she indicated that I should do the same. He weighed almost nothing and between us we steadied him for the walk around the verandah to my room.

'Rest here,' Mrs Fagan said, and sat the poor man on my bed. Then she turned to me. 'Gather up ya things, lass. Florrie can be makin' up a camp bed for ya.'

While I packed my few belongings into my travel bag, Mrs Fagan took off Mr Hannan's boots. She lifted his legs and swung them up onto the bed.

'I'll be bringin' ya some water,' she told him, although I don't think he heard her. His eyes had closed again. His skin had a sort of waxy look to it and every breath he took sounded as if it would be his last.

'Get out yer doctor book, Clara,' Mrs Fagan said quietly. 'I'm after thinkin' he may have typhoid.'

'Typhoid!' I exclaimed.

'Hush now, lass,' Mrs Fagan whispered, her finger resting across her lips. 'Ya'll be scarin' the livin' daylights outta him.'

I suspected there was not much 'daylight' left in him by then, but I took the encyclopaedia out of my bag. Mrs

Fagan made a shooing motion and we stepped outside onto the verandah. I looked up typhoid fever in the book and began to read:

> *A severe infection caused by the bacterium* Salmonella typhi *being ingested into the stomach and passed into the stool or urine.*
> Causes: *Eating or drinking food or water contaminated by flies, poor hygiene or lack of sanitation.*
> Treatment: *Plenty of fluids, bed rest, plain rice.*
> NB: *Highly contagious.*

During that first day, I looked in on Mr Hannan as often as I could. Eventually I woke him and supported his head while I held a mug of boiled water to his lips. He took a mouthful and swallowed it eagerly, then slumped back and closed his eyes again. His skin was hot and damp to touch. He had taken off his shirt and a pinkish rash showed above the neckline of his flannel undershirt. I put a bucket beside his bed and went out quietly.

In the evening I tried to feed him some plain boiled rice. He chewed a little but couldn't swallow it. He retched painfully and the mush ran down his chin and onto his flannel which was already soaked with sweat. He lay back, exhausted. I cleaned him up and let him rest. He looked so bad that first night that I expected him to be dead before long.

The next morning I went into the room to find Paddy Hannan lying motionless in the bed with his eyes closed. To my surprise, he was still breathing. I took out the bucket and put the empty chamber-pot from under his bed in its place. When I put water on his lips he licked them, but did not seem to be aware that I was there.

I continued to check on him as I went about my work. In the evening, when I opened his door, I could see that he was awake.

'How are you, Mr Hannan?' I asked. He tried to speak but it was only after I had spooned some of the boiled water into his mouth that any sound came out.

'Better ... I think.' His voice was so faint that I had to lean in to hear him. There was a sickly sweet smell to his breath. He tried to sit up, but his elbows wouldn't support him. I put some more water on a spoon and he opened his dry lips eagerly. Some of the water trickled out of the corner of his mouth. I wiped it away and tucked the handtowel under his chin before I offered him more. When most of the water was gone, he closed his eyes. I straightened out his bedding as best I could.

'Remind me of your name, lass,' he said faintly as I bent to tuck the sheet around him. His flannel now stank of dried sweat and the smell of his body almost made me gag.

'Clara,' I told him, straightening up. 'Clara Saunders.'

'Thank you, Clara,' he said. I left him then. There was nothing more I could do.

# MAY 1893

For the next two days I took water to Mr Hannan, emptied and cleaned out his chamber-pot and made him as comfortable as possible. There was very little change in him, although when he was awake he would say that he felt better.

Tobias's Store did sell a remedy called Mrs Watson's Stomach Powder, which claimed to cure all stomach disorders, when taken with water. Mrs Fagan said it was just cornflour in a fancy box, but I thought it was worth trying. And we had plenty of rice in the pantry. If I boiled some up to make it soft enough for Mr Hannan to eat and added the powder, perhaps he could keep a little of it down. I remembered Mother feeding us freshly grated apple when we were ill, but fresh fruit was extremely rare in Coolgardie.

By Wednesday morning I was convinced that there was an improvement. Mr Hannan's breathing was steadier and the whites of his eyes were almost clear.

'You are looking much better today,' I told him, and hurried back to the kitchen to try out my rice idea.

⁂

Over the next ten days Mr Hannan's health slowly improved. He told me that he had been prospecting further east and had found some 'colour', but his supplies had run low. On his way back into Coolgardie to pick up more stores, a hole had developed in his waterbag. In desperation he scooped up some muddy water from a clay pan and drank it.

When Paddy Hannan was strong enough to sit up, he talked to me about his travels. He was a very successful prospector and knew how to survive in dry country. He had been prospecting in remote areas of the Kimberley and all over Australia. He'd lived in some of the same places as us – Bathurst, Ballarat, Bendigo, Charters Towers. I told him that my father and brothers were still in Queensland and he knew of Cooper's Mine, where they worked. I hadn't heard from them in a long time, although Mother sometimes received letters from Pa. She knew how much I missed him and always passed on his love to me through Jack or Mr Snell. Her own writing was not as steady as it used to be, but Susan wrote to me most weeks. She said that Mother was well, but starting to show her age. I wrote back when I could, but after working all day I sometimes fell asleep with the pencil in my hand.

I could see Paddy Hannan getting stronger, day by day, which made me feel good about taking him in. I would be sad to see him go when the time came, but the prospect of having my room back was something I did look forward to. Bunking in with Florrie was fun, but there was not much space. I had never had a room of my own before and I did miss it.

Although Florrie was seven years older than me, she was easy to talk to and good company. She was still getting used to things like heat and dust and flies, but she was most unhappy when the camel trains didn't arrive on time and we ran short of food. In spite of her dainty figure, Florrie was always hungry.

'No bread again today?' she said. I shook my head. Florrie lifted down the biscuit tin from the mantle shelf above the stove and prised the lid off. 'And only three oat biscuits left!' she exclaimed. 'What are we going to do?'

'Tobias might be able to find some more rolled oats in his storeroom somewhere,' I said, not holding out much hope. The whole town had been waiting since the end of April for Abdul's team of camels to arrive with the supplies. It was now three weeks overdue.

'If he doesn't come today, I'll be forced to eat my boot leather,' Florrie wailed.

'We've tried to get a message to Mr Snell, but his coach is only set up for passengers. Even if he made a special trip out here, he couldn't bring enough flour for the whole town.'

'Tell him I'll pay him double – triple, anything he asks,' Florrie declared.

'At least we have eggs,' I tried to console her. 'Although even the chooks' oats are getting low. They may not keep laying if we use up all their food to make our biscuits.'

'I'm glad I wasn't here when the first rush was on,' she said. 'I can't imagine how anyone survived.'

'It wasn't easy,' I told her. 'People shared what they had.'

'What about the greedy ones?'

'Do you know,' I said, 'I can't remember them.'

*

While I was bunking in with Florrie, she took to joining me on my morning walks. In spite of her occasional grumpiness she was interested in everything. Like me, she loved the cool early mornings.

'I wish I was a painter,' she said one day as we watched the sun come up over the corrugated sand plain. 'The colours out here at this time of day are unbelievably beautiful.'

We sat for a while, watching the changing patterns of light and shadow, relaxing in the cool air and comfortable silence. Then we headed back to town to face the busy day ahead.

# JUNE 1893

The weather was still dry but the days were getting shorter and the nights were freezing. Some mornings, when I went into the kitchen before setting off on my walk, the wet hessian strips that hung down the sides of the Coolgardie Safe were frozen stiff.

One morning in early June, when I went in to do the room for Mr Hannan I found him packing his swag. 'Ah, Clara,' he said, 'I have somethin' for ya here.'

I wondered what it could be. Mr Hannan had barely left the room since he arrived. 'Ya've taken good care of me, Clara,' he said. 'I owe ya me life, I know that.' He opened the top drawer in the bedside chest and lifted something out. 'This is the first nugget I found out there on me new show,' he said, and unwrapped the cloth from around it. 'It ain't worth a lot now, but it has brought me luck.' He took my hand, turned it over, and placed a stone in my open palm. 'I'm hopin' it will do the same for ya,' he said. Lying there in my hand was a nugget of pure gold.

'It's beautiful,' I gasped. 'But I can't accept it.'

'Please,' he said. 'Ya've earned it ten times over and I will be mightily offended if ya will not do me just one more favour.' He closed the fingers of my hand over the nugget. 'Take care now, Clara.'

He went out into the courtyard, crossed to the stables, and I never saw him again. But I heard about him. It would not be long before the whole world knew about Paddy Hannan.

*

In the middle of June, Mr Wisdom came striding into the dining room.

'Paddy Hannan's back in town!' he shouted. 'His new claim is even bigger than Bayley's!' We all stopped what we were doing. There were a few early drinkers at the bar. They swung around to look at Mr Wisdom. 'A reef of pure gold, a good mile long and just twenty-eight miles east of here!'

A clamour of voices started up. People came in off the street to find out what was happening. They looked at each other in disbelief.

'Blimey.'

'Aeh, ye're havin' us on.'

'There's never gunna be one bigger than Bayley's.'

'Fair dinkum,' Mr Wisdom said. 'I'm telling you.'

The bar began to empty. Men hurried back to their camps to pack their gear.

'Will there be a new rush?' I asked Mr Wisdom.

'Nothing surer,' he said. 'Let's just hope they've found water out there, as well as gold. Men will be dropping like flies otherwise.'

*

By the end of the week, many of the camps had gone. Coolgardie was not the end of the line any more. Now there was passing traffic to cater for, as well as the remaining locals.

A few weeks later another hotel sprang up. Florrie and I were pleased to have a little less work to do, but there was fierce rivalry between the two pubs. The days when everyone in the town knew each other were over. There were con men, prostitutes and criminals on the run, mostly passing through but causing plenty of trouble as they went. Since October 1892, when Coolgardie officially became a town, it had gained a reputation as a frontier community with remarkably little crime, but that was changing.

*

Soon after that Mr Wisdom appeared in the kitchen with a rifle. While my body automatically tensed, my mind refused to believe what I saw.

'We already have meat for the dinner tonight, Mr Wisdom.' I grinned at the awkward way he carried the rifle. He was fiercely opposed to hunting wildlife – even though, when we first arrived, we would not have survived without killing some of the kangaroos for meat.

'I'm not going hunting, Clara,' he said. 'But I am getting worried. You and Florrie, even Mrs Fagan, are quite vulnerable out the back here when the bar is full. There's a rougher crowd in town these days.'

I stared at him. Surely none of us were in any more danger of being molested than we had always been. We all knew how to defend ourselves and none of us had gold claims of our own. I had hidden Paddy Hannan's nugget in my bottom drawer, but he had said it wasn't worth much. It was precious to me, but hardly worth stealing.

'You are probably perfectly safe,' Mr Wisdom said, although he seemed to be trying to convince himself rather than me. At that point Mrs Fagan came in.

'And what are ya doin' with that?' she demanded. 'Sure, ya'll be shootin' yerself in the foot, carryin' a weapon that way!'

'I'm mindful of your safety, Mrs Fagan,' he shuffled his feet, looking a bit embarrassed, then leaned the rifle in the corner behind the stove. 'And that of the two young ladies in your care.'

Mrs Fagan let out a great shout of laughter, which brought Florrie in to see what was going on. 'In my care?' the housekeeper was saying. ''Tis more like them carin' for me, now. But sure, we've no need of a rifle. We have tricks aplenty for dealin' with yon larrikins.' She tapped her temple with one finger. ''Tis what's up here that'll be keepin' us safe, thank ya kindly.' She took her chopping board from where it stood draining on the bench, and picked up the meat cleaver. 'With maybe a little help from this here,' she shook the cleaver playfully in Mr Wisdom's direction. He said no more. But the rifle remained where he had placed it.

Florrie and I walked around the verandah together. 'God help any no-good shyster who thinks he can get the better of Mrs Fagan,' she said.

'Or you,' I said. 'You may look as if a puff of wind would blow you over, but I know different.'

She laughed and danced back to her work, spreading her arms as if she was indeed being carried by the wind.

# NOVEMBER 1893

Towards the end of one of the hottest days in the summer after Paddy Hannan's find, one of the regulars at the hotel, Bluey Whitehead, came in from his outlying camp. He had taken off his shirt, which was drenched in sweat, and wore it tied around his waist when he appeared at the kitchen door.

'Bar's that way,' Florrie told him. He didn't move. 'Or is it the office you need?'

'No, miss,' he said, snatching the battered hat off his head and holding it pressed to his chest. 'I come for Miss Clara.'

'What is it, Bluey?' I asked, wiping my hands down my apron.

'Bill Derby is took real bad, miss,' he said.

'Did you take him to the nurses' tent?' I asked. Four nurses had arrived and set up a sick bay in a tent on the edge of town, with proper equipment and medicines. They were working night and day, doing what they could for the sick and injured, even though many of the old bushmen wouldn't go near them. They had an unshakeable fear of ending their days in a hospital.

'He won't come in,' Bluey said. 'I fear if you don't come out to him, he'll not last the night.'

'How far out are you?' Florrie asked.

'Five miles,' Bluey said.

'Five miles! In this heat,' Florrie said, shaking her head, but Bluey's eyes never left mine.

'Please, miss, he knows you from all the time he spends at the pub. He'll listen to you.' The man looked so desperate that my heart went out to him.

'I'll have to finish up here and –'

'I'll wait,' he said. A look of relief swept the lines from his face. He beamed and backed out of the doorway.

'You can't walk five miles in this heat,' Florrie declared.

'I'll manage,' I said, taking my hat from the peg and downing a glass of water.

'Wait. I'm coming too,' Florrie said.

I stopped and looked at her. 'Are you sure?' I asked. Florrie's fair English skin never tanned and she suffered badly in this sort of weather.

She took her hat from the peg and jammed it on her head. 'Shall we go?' she said, glaring at me and marching out the door.

⁂

It was mid-afternoon. There was not a breath of wind and no obvious drop in the temperature. We had gone about a mile when Florrie turned to me and said, 'This is madness.

We'll die of heat stroke and where will that leave your mate Bill Derby?'

'It is hot,' I agreed. 'But I can't let him die out there.'

Florrie and I trudged along behind Bluey. My dress clung to my back and I gave up trying to wipe the sweat and flies from my face. We passed a low mallee tree and I broke off a switch of leaves. It did little to shift the flies, but at least it created a slight movement in the air as I swung it back and forth. I broke off another one and handed it to Florrie. I swapped my bag, packed with towels, patent medicines and my mother's book, from one shoulder to the other, not only because it was heavy, but to cool the sweaty patch on my dress underneath. In spite of me telling Florrie not to come, I was glad of her company.

'Not far now, miss,' Bluey turned his head to reassure us.

We finally reached a rough bush hut. It was surrounded by rubbish. Everything was covered in the usual layer of red dust. Nothing moved. Even the old dog lying in the shade appeared, at first, to be dead. It eventually opened one eye, but did not get up. Bluey put his head in through the open door, then turned and beckoned to us. 'You'll be all right now, Bill,' Bluey said cheerfully. 'Miss Clara has come to help you.'

I stepped inside the one-room hut. Even in the dim light, the mess was confronting. Soiled clothing lay on the dirt floor beside the bed. The mattress had been discarded and a single filthy sheet covered the sagging canvas that was stretched over an iron bed frame. I glanced at Florrie, who had followed me in. I could see she was struggling not to vomit.

Bill Derby lay inert on the bed. When he opened his eyes they seemed far too big for his shrunken face. The tattered flannel singlet that hung loosely on his body was covered in sweat and grime. He wore no trousers. Bluey quickly pulled the flannel down over his friend's crotch. The shape of each bone in his legs showed clearly under the wrinkled flesh.

'Go away,' he croaked through parched lips. 'I don't want no women messin' about wi' me.'

'Oh, yes you do, Bill Derby,' I said. 'You love women. And we've come all the way out here to see you. Now let's get this flannel off and give you a wash.'

Bill turned his head away. 'I ain't havin' no wash. Washin' weakens a man.' Out of the corner of his eye, he glared at Florrie. 'Get her outta here,' he demanded.

'Oh, I'm more than happy to oblige, you ungrateful old sod,' Florrie almost spat the words at him. An empty wooden box stood just inside the doorway. She picked it up, marched out with it, set it against the wall in a patch of shade and sat there fanning herself with her hat.

'Now, Bill, don't you go upsettin' these ladies.' Bluey came in with a kerosene tin that had been converted into a bucket. I frowned as I peered inside it. 'Water for washin',' Bluey explained. 'It's only been used once.'

I took out a washcloth from my bag and dipped it in the milky-looking water. Bill's skin was so hot to touch that I didn't need a thermometer to tell me he had a raging fever. I suspected typhoid, but I knew I wouldn't be able to treat him properly out in the camps if it was.

'Where's your drinking water?' I asked Bluey.

A makeshift Coolgardie safe stood in the corner. He opened it and took out a pottery jug.

'Has this water been boiled?' I said. Bluey nodded and I held the jug to Bill's lips. At first, he tried to push it away, but Bluey pinned down his arms, and I kept coaxing him to try it. Eventually Bill gulped down a mouthful of water.

I washed the filth and grime from Bill's body and decided not to dry him. I was hoping the evaporating water would lower his temperature a little. I waited for several minutes. Bill's eyes closed but his limbs looked more relaxed. In spite of his protests it seemed the bathing had made him more comfortable. I offered the jug of water again. This time he drank deeply.

I found Bluey and Florrie sitting together outside in the shade of the hut. The dog had moved slightly to make room for them.

'You'll have to bring him into town, Bluey. His temperature is coming down, but he really needs the doctor,' I said.

'He won't go!' Bluey shook his head. 'I've tried to make him. He just says he ain't goin' nowhere. He'd rather die here.'

'I'll get Mac to come out with his donkey cart. When he arrives, you and Mac will have to pick Bill up and get him into it. He's in no state to put up a fight. Just be firm with him, Bluey.' The old prospector sucked in his bottom lip, but nodded his head. 'Take him to the nurses,' I insisted. 'They'll have a bed for him. Then find Doctor Foreman.' The doctor had recently moved into town, but was often called out to the nurses' tent.

'Right, miss.' Bluey stood up and straightened his shoulders. For a moment, I thought he might leap to attention. I felt a giggle coming on in spite of everything, or maybe because of it. After the relentless heat, the long walk and the effort of trying to help a man who didn't want my help, I didn't know whether to laugh or cry.

*

'Will he recover?' Florrie asked as we made our way slowly back to town. I felt drained of every last ounce of energy and could barely place one foot in front of the other. I simply shrugged and spread my hands.

The sun had set by the time Florrie and I reached the hotel, but there was still no cooling easterly wind. We went into the kitchen, took off our hats and flopped down onto the chairs. Florrie took off her shoes and stretched her legs straight out in front of her. I dumped my boots and folded my body forward, resting my aching head in my hands.

Mrs Fagan took the jug from the Coolgardie safe and poured a glass of water for each of us. As usual, in really hot weather, she had a wet cotton handkerchief draped around the back of her neck. She kept taking it off, dipping it in a bowl of washing water, and putting it in place again. It kept her cool, she said, although her face was so red and her brow so sweaty that I wondered if it had any effect at all.

'Is old Bill Derby still alive, then?' Mrs Fagan asked, sitting down and lifting her skirts to fan herself with them.

'Barely,' I said.

'Cantankerous as ever, I'll be bound,' she muttered.

'I don't think he's eaten in days,' I told her. 'He's in a desperate state.'

'And filthy,' Florrie added, holding her nose.

'His clothes are so ragged they're falling off him,' I said. 'He needs a new shirt and flannel at the very least.'

'Aeh, lass, just leave that to me now,' Mrs Fagan winked. 'I'm thinkin' that our friend Evan Wisdom will be after losin' another one of his shirts in the wash, so he will.'

'Mrs Fagan!' Florrie sounded shocked. 'You haven't stolen Mr Wisdom's shirts before, have you?'

'Well now, he's plenty of 'em,' she said. 'And he'll not really mind, even if he does miss it. I'll be after choosin' one he doesn't wear.'

Florrie and I looked at each other and laughed. It was the best pick-me-up we could possibly have had.

# DECEMBER 1893

'Florrie!' I called as I ran into the kitchen. She looked up. 'Mr Faahan's piano has arrived at last! He's going to put on a ball at his hotel, for Boxing Day. Won't that be such great fun!' I had expected Florrie to join me in the waltz I was doing around the kitchen. She put a slight smile on her face, but I could see that it was only because she thought my dancing was funny. 'What's the matter?' I asked. The smile disappeared.

'Oh, Clara, I don't have anything to wear to a ball, and I can't stand this any longer.'

'What?'

'Everything. The heat, the flies, the "dunnies" – I've had enough of living rough. I've decided to leave Coolgardie.'

Her words hit me like a punch in the gut. All my excitement escaped through my open mouth.

'I'll miss you,' I said when I got my breath back. 'Anyway, I'm the same as you. The soles of my shoes have gone through and if Mother doesn't send me some soon, I'll be completely barefooted.'

Florrie's smile came creeping back. 'I saw some brand-new leather bluchers in Tobias's Store the other day,' she said.

'And I'm sure you would just love to see me trying to dance in men's shoes!' I pulled a face at her. 'Please stay, Florrie.' I squatted down in front of her chair and took her hands in mine.

At first, she wouldn't look at me. Then she said, 'All right. I'll stay until after the ball.'

I leapt up, pulled her to her feet and whirled her around the room.

'Away,' Mrs Fagan said, shooing us out of the kitchen. 'Ye'll be upsettin' me trays, so ye will, and I can't be startin' again with these biscuits.'

⁂

Everyone was talking about the ball. Consignments of fine lace, linen, even lengths of silk arrived at Tobias's. The women were all busy sewing, altering dresses or making new ones. Dressy shoes were rare in Coolgardie, so bows and colourful ribbons were being added to make their boots look a little more glamorous.

Christmas drew closer and we baked extra batches of biscuits and cakes so that some could be set aside for supper at the ball.

⁂

I hadn't seen Jack for six weeks and I missed him terribly. There were so many things I wanted to talk with him about. When I asked Mr Snell, he said Jack and his father were often out of town working. They were finding it hard to keep their business going since the levels in their dams and soaks were at an all-time low.

'I was hoping he would be here for the ball,' I said.

'Perhaps he hasn't heard about it,' Mr Snell replied. 'Write him a letter.'

I did, but I heard nothing from Jack.

*

On Christmas Eve, Florrie and I joined in the usual singalong in the dining room. Dryblower Murphy was there, leading the singing and keeping everyone entertained. He had come from Victoria to try his luck in the west and immediately fitted into the town. He was a poet and storyteller with a great singing voice. Florrie's sweet soprano blended well with his strong tenor and he suggested that they sing a duet.

'Oh, no. I couldn't,' Florrie was shaking her head, but shouts of encouragement and drumming on tables convinced her to say yes. After a short consultation, they sang the folk song 'Scarborough Fair'. The hushed crowd swayed in time until their voices died away with 'Then she'll be a true love of mine.' Amongst the applause there were murmurs of, 'We wish', shouts for Dryblower to recite his latest bush ballad, then calls for Padraig to tell us some of his Irish jokes.

'Have ye heard the one about the Englishman travellin' through County Cork?' Padraig asked his audience.

'Sure ya're goin' to tell us anyway. Get on with it, Padraig.'

'The Englishman sees a farmer comin' along the road

towards him,' Padraig began, ignoring the banter from his mates. '"Excuse me, my good man,"' Padraig said, putting on a posh English accent. '"Can you tell me how to get to Limerick?" The farmer takes off his hat and scratches his head. He looks up and down the road. Then, shakin' his head sadly, the farmer says, "Ah, well, I'd like to help ya, so I would, but if I were goin' to Limerick, now, I wouldn't be startin' from here."'

There were shouts of laughter. Someone called out, 'That's an old one, Padraig.' Someone else yelled, 'Aye, but a good one, so.'

'Worth a drink, anyways,' Padraig yelled back, and someone handed him a glass of beer.

*

It was getting late and I still had to sew on some lace I had bought to make my good dress look a bit more festive. I said goodnight to Florrie and headed towards my room. There was no moon, but as I came out through the kitchen I saw a familiar shape on the verandah.

'Jack!' I ran to him and he hugged me tight. When I leaned back in his arms and looked at him, I saw that he was wearing a bow tie and a new waistcoat.

'Don't you say anything,' he warned, and placed his finger across my lips. Then he stepped back and made a bow. 'Miss Clara Saunders, will you do me the honour of being my partner at the Boxing Day ball?'

I wanted so much to laugh, but I pulled my face as straight as I could.

'Mr Raeside,' I said. 'I am delighted to accept your invitation.'

'Phew,' he sighed, and the tension went out of his body. 'I was afraid you might already be spoken for.'

'You're lucky I'm not,' I said. 'When you didn't answer my letter, I thought you'd ditched me.'

'What letter?' Jack asked.

'Never mind. You're here now and I can't wait for Boxing Day. We'll have to bring Florrie, though. She's been a bit down lately. She's decided to leave.'

'Florrie?' Jack looked worried. 'Why is she leaving?'

'She says she's sick of heat and dust and flies,' I said.

Jack nodded. 'It must be hard. So different from England.'

'I persuaded her to stay until after the ball,' I said, 'but I'll miss her so much.'

Jack took both of my hands in his. 'Hey, cheer up,' he said. 'It might not happen.'

'You're right,' I said, feeling the smile spreading across my face. It was so good to see him. I looked him up and down. 'My, you are formal tonight.'

'I need to break in these new clothes. This tie is killing me,' he said, running his finger around inside the collar of his white shirt.

'Now you've made it go crooked,' I told him, and reached up to set it straight. There was a faint smell of starch and shaving cream about him. Combined with the new clothes, it made him seem different, distant even.

'Thanks,' he said. 'I can't dance if I'm not comfortable. Oh, I nearly forgot. I have something for you.'

I tilted my head and looked at him curiously while he stooped down and picked up a box from the verandah. It was wrapped in brown paper and tied with string. I felt the weight of it, shook it to see if it rattled and turned it over. Something moved inside as I tugged at the string.

'Come into the kitchen,' I said. 'I can't see out here.'

The kitchen was deserted, but coals still glowed in the fireplace. I brought the lamp down from its shelf and lit the wick with a taper. With Mrs Fagan's sharp knife, I cut the string on the parcel. The brown paper fell away and I opened the box.

'New shoes! From Mother!' I hugged Jack and did a little dance, then brought the shoes to my nose and breathed in the wonderful smell of new leather. They were a deep burgundy colour, easy to keep clean in our red-brown town. Best of all, when I turned the shoes over in my hands, I saw the elegant tapered heel. These were the first pair of real shoes I had ever had; practical, but stylish, and so much lighter than my working boots.

'Perfect!' I exclaimed.

⁂

Christmas Day was so busy that it passed in a blur for me. All the regulars came into the hotel for Christmas dinner and we did our best to provide traditional fare. A dozen chickens had been killed and plucked the day before. Potatoes and pumpkins were roasted in the fat and served with large quantities of Mrs Fagan's famous gravy. We had made the Christmas puddings a week before because there was not enough room on the stove to cook everything at once. The heat in the kitchen at midday was so intense that although we had planned to reheat the puddings, we decided to just pour the hot custard over them. The dried fruit had softened while the puddings sat resting in their calico wrappings. The flavours of cinnamon and nutmeg, glazed cherries and candied peel had spread through them and produced a wonderfully moist, mouth-watering pudding. Florrie said she had never tasted better, even in England.

By Christmas night we were all exhausted and Mr Wisdom decided that, with the ball the following evening, he would not open the hotel until midday. We could sleep in for an extra hour in the morning and still get our chores done in time.

# DECEMBER 1893

Boxing Day seemed to drag by. I couldn't wait for eight o'clock, but I was nervous, too. I had been looking forward to the ball so much that, now that it was almost here, I worried that something would go wrong and spoil it.

At last the sun went down and the temperature began to drop. Jack arrived in his white shirt and waistcoat. It was too hot to wear his jacket, but he carried it slung over his shoulder.

'I was looking for Clara. Have you seen her anywhere?' Jack teased as I stepped out to meet him in my lace-trimmed dress and new shoes.

'Lucky you needed your tie straightened the other night, or I wouldn't have recognised you either,' I said as Jack offered me his arm.

As we passed Florrie's room, I called to her, 'Are you ready?'

'Won't be a minute. You go on,' she called from behind the door.

'We can wait,' Jack called back. 'Mind you, I've never known a woman who can be ready in one minute. I'll wager five pounds it will take longer than that.'

The door opened and there was Florrie. Her hair was piled up and pinned in curls on the top of her head. Her best dress was washed and pressed. She had even contrived to add a white lace collar that showed off her smooth English skin.

'Florrie, you look wonderful!' I exclaimed. 'I thought you didn't have anything to wear.'

'So did I,' Florrie said, and did a pirouette to show off the matching lace she had sewn around the hem of her full skirt.

❋

The dining rooms at the Club Hotel were beautifully decorated with coloured streamers, artificial silk flowers and fresh leafy boughs of gum and kurrajong. The local gum trees were so tall and spindly that ladders must have been taken out onto the plain specially to reach the high branches. It was worth the effort, though. A pleasant smell of eucalyptus filled the spacious rooms. Unlike our Exchange Hotel, which had struggled up out of nothing and grown bit by bit, this hotel had been built to accommodate a crowd.

Dancing with Jack, our bodies moving easily together and our steps matching effortlessly, I looked around the room. It was full of old friends and new acquaintances. Florrie, Mrs Fagan, the warden and Mrs Finnerty, Padraig,

Jock and Mac. Jock and Mac came here on Mr Snell's coach with me, but I felt as if I had known them forever. Dryblower Murphy had arrived since then, and become part of our lives. Dryblower wrote some very funny bush ballads and sometimes read them out to entertain the crowd in the bar. He had to compete with Henry Lawson and Banjo Paterson for column inches in *The Bulletin*, but we felt he was one of our own and understood the goldfields better than most.

The women were dressed in the finest clothes I had ever seen in Coolgardie. Everyone was laughing, talking, relaxing, dancing, enjoying each other's company. I felt happier that night than ever before in my life. I thought of Mother saying she hoped I would not come to regret leaving Southern Cross. If only she could see me now. At that moment there was nothing more I could wish for.

*

After midnight, the crowd began to thin out. With six or more men to every woman, Florrie and I were in big demand as dancing partners, but Jack made sure he didn't miss out. We danced until two a.m. and I still wasn't the least bit tired. While the band took a break, people gathered around the keg and began to sing. Jack and Dryblower Murphy provided the harmony while the rest of us joined in.

A cool easterly wind had been blowing for several hours but it was still hot inside.

'Let's go outside and cool off,' Jack said eventually. He took off his tie and undid the top button of his shirt. I didn't want this special night to end, so we sat out on the verandah where we could still hear the music. The black dome of the sky was studded with stars. They looked so close in the clear, dry air that I felt I could reach up and catch one. Jack took the handkerchief out of his pocket and wiped the sweat off his face. At that moment a comet came streaking across the sky.

'Jack, look!' I tapped his arm. 'A shooting star.' He pulled the handkerchief away from his eyes. We both stared up at the sky, but the fast-moving ball of light with its fiery tail had all but disappeared. 'Make a wish,' I said.

'Damn. I missed it,' he replied, but put his arm around my shoulders. I leaned against him, looked up at the sky and smiled. My wish had already been granted.

⁕

It was three a.m. before the ball was finally over. The exhausted musicians packed up their instruments and the last of the dancers trickled out into the night. Florrie had stayed to the end and the three of us walked back to the Exchange Hotel together. Jack said goodnight and went to join Tobias, who had offered him a place to sleep for the night on the floor of one of his storerooms.

⁕

Over breakfast the next morning, Florrie asked me, 'Are you in love with Jack?' I was still not properly awake and stopped eating to think about it. 'Just asking,' Florrie said before taking a sip of her tea and crunching into another piece of toast with jam.

'Jack and I are best mates,' I said, eventually. 'You can't be in love with your best mate, can you?'

'Of course not,' Florrie agreed. 'A best mate is, well... a best mate.'

We talked about Padraig, who was a good friend of Jack's, as well as mine, and Arthur Williams, who was always so kind to me, but sometimes looked at me strangely.

'You mean the way Dryblower Murphy looks at me?' Florrie laughed.

'Well, yes, I suppose so. But Arthur is much older.'

'How old is Jack?' Florrie asked.

'Twenty,' I said. We talked about other things, but at the back of my mind I was still thinking about whether I was in love with Jack. We had fierce arguments and there were long periods when we didn't see each other, but we always seemed to fit back together as if we had never been apart. I loved Mother, and Pa, and Susan, in a different way. She often made me so angry I could shake her, but I knew that if anything bad happened to her I would be awfully upset. Emily was fun, but she and Mary were grown-ups, nearly twice my age. I liked them, but I hardly knew them. And the boys were almost alien creatures, needing no-one but each other. I realised that Jack was different. I knew him and he knew me. He saw through my skin, right into my soul. But being in love – that seemed to imply marriage, which, to my mind, was nowhere near as much fun as being best mates.

# JANUARY 1894

Jack moved to Coolgardie to try being a prospector. He bought a tent with the wages his father had paid him, added a pick and shovel, tinned provisions, dry biscuits, then a hat with a fly net and corks hanging around the brim. I laughed out loud when he tried on the hat in Tobias's Store.

'I look the part, then?' he said, squashing the hat down more firmly on his head.

'You look like a bushwhacker,' I told him. 'Where is that dashing young man who was wearing a tie at the ball?'

He swung the shovel up onto his shoulder like a rifle, clicked his heels together and stood to attention. 'At your service, ma'am,' he said, with a lopsided salute.

'Go easy with that weapon, mate!' A man with a brand-new wheelbarrow was trying to get through between Jack and the stacks of boxes that were blocking the aisle.

'Sorry,' Jack said, stepping aside. With the hat still on his head, he took his gear to the counter.

'Suits you, Jack,' Tobias grinned. I tried to keep a straight face.

While Jack paid the bill I tried to imagine how it would be for him living away from his mother, who doted on him, and trying to scratch a living out of Coolgardie's fickle patch of dirt. Would he get bored with it? Would he struggle to survive without regular wages from his father? I had been looking forward to him coming, but what if he hated it?

I went back to work, expecting to see Jack that evening, but several days passed. Where was he? I was beginning to worry. Had something happened to him, out there in his tent? I asked several people if they had seen him. No-one had. I told myself not to be silly, that of course he was all right. He was an experienced bushman and knew this country well.

Another day went by. I had made up my mind to walk out to his tent before work the next morning when I saw Jack in the dining room. He had dragged a chair over and sat down at a table with Jock, Mac and some of his new mates like Bill Lockhart. I delivered more meals to the counter and paused on the way back to speak to Jack.

'Where have you been?' I asked.

'What?' The room was so crowded and noisy with men talking, laughing and shouting their greetings while plates and cutlery clashed and clattered.

'I was worried.'

Jack looked at me blankly. He turned one ear towards me and cupped his hand behind it.

'I was worried,' I shouted, bending towards him.

'Why?'

'It's what friends do,' I said. Jack looked puzzled. 'We are still friends, aren't we?' I asked.

Shouting broke out at the next table. Men demanding their meals began to clash with others calling for drinks.

'Wait your turn!' I shouted above the din.

'You're busy. I'll get out of your way,' Jack said, and stood up to go. The table rocked, spilling a man's drink. 'Sorry, mate,' Jack bent down quickly to speak to him. Men had been killed in pubs for less, but not in this one. 'I'll get you another,' Jack said, and brushed past me on his way to the bar.

'Jack!' He held up one hand and continued pushing through the crowd. My temper blazed. 'Suit yourself, Jack Raeside, but don't expect me to be waiting!' He pulled a sheepish face but that only made me angrier. I glared at him, but he was hailing Mr Wisdom, ordering the new drink. I dodged the scuffle that had broken out and marched off towards the kitchen.

It was hot. I was tired and irritated, fed up with always having to deal with demanding men.

When I came back with the next lot of meals, Jack was gone. As I passed their table, I heard Mac say, 'That dingo is on the prowl again. Cleaned out all Jack's food.'

'He'll be wantin' some barrels then – with lids,' Jock said. 'Leavin' them opened tins of food around out there, that's like offerin' a free feed to every livin' creature within miles.'

'Yeah, old whisky barrels with lids. That'll do the trick,' Bill Lockhart said. 'And I'm his man. I could be a real gentleman and help him with the emptyin' of 'em.' That set off a chorus of other voices chipping in with offers of help to empty a barrel of whisky.

⁂

For the rest of the evening I looked for Jack every time I came into the dining room. If a dingo had stolen his food, he would be hungry. He had to eat. Where else could he go? I was tired before, but now it felt like something heavy in my chest was weighing me down. What was Jack doing? I needed him to come back so that I could say sorry.

This was not how I had imagined things would be now that Jack was living here. Somehow he seemed further away than when he lived in Southern Cross. And Florrie's questions about being in love had unsettled me. I needed to talk to Jack, but I was already feeling squeezed out of his new life.

When I had finished cleaning up in the kitchen, I set the bread dough to rise on the hob, took off my apron and flopped down in a chair.

'Are you all right?' Florrie asked as she took the jug from the cooler and poured herself a drink of water.

I nodded and tried to smile. 'I'm completely done in,' I said. 'I'll see you in the morning.'

'Goodnight, then,' she said, giving me a curious look as she went out into the night.

I sat for a while, thinking about things. When I opened the Coolgardie safe to pour myself a cool drink, I noticed that the water trays at the top and bottom of the metal safe were dry. The heat in the kitchen had been fierce all day and the wet hessian that hung down its perforated sides had dried out.

When I had quenched my thirst and calmed myself, I carried the trays outside and refilled them at the water tank. Jack was not waiting on the verandah.

The trays were tricky to balance when they were full of water and I spilled some on the kitchen floor. I could have left it to dry overnight, but I brought the mop in from outside the door and washed the floor with the spilled water. Even though it was late by the time I finished, Jack was still not there.

Arthur Williams was behind the bar, adding up the takings for the day.

'Have you seen Jack?' I asked.

Arthur looked up from the line of figures he was working on. 'Everyone's gone home,' he said. 'But I'll come for a stroll with you, if you like.'

'Thank you kindly, Arthur, but I'm very tired,' I said, and went to my room.

# JANUARY 1894

I couldn't sleep. I was dog-tired but the room was hot and stuffy. I tossed and turned in my narrow bed. My mouth was dry again so I got up, lit my lamp and carried it to the kitchen. The cool night air caressed my bare arms. A puff of wind swirled around my legs, lifting the threadbare linen of my nightdress and soothing my hot skin. Stars filled the sky. Their brightness made it look even more intensely black. The sad face of the moon looked down.

I began to wish that I could take back the harsh words I had said to Jack, but I was still angry with him for brushing me off and leaving the pub without saying goodnight. Nothing was working out as I had expected. Was Jack changing, or was I the one who was seeing things in a different way? Was I in love with Jack after all? I wanted to ask my mother. Suddenly I felt a long way from home.

The jug in the cooler was less than half full. I took a long drink and refilled it with boiled water from the kettle on the hob. Then I went back to bed. Half an hour later I was up again, going out the back to the dunny.

When I came back, the calico square covering my window was moving gently in and out. As I drifted into sleep, I made up my mind to visit Jack's camp in the morning.

⁂

I was awake even before the cockatoos in the trees made their first announcements of the day. Jack's camp was well out on a different track to the one I usually took on my morning walk, but I gathered up some storage tins with lids. Mrs Fagan had said I could lend them to Jack. With the tins clinking together in a sack slung over my shoulder, I set off towards his camp. The sack grew heavy and awkward on my back. I stopped several times to shift it from one shoulder to the other. The sun was well up above the horizon by the time I reached Jack's tent. There was no sign of movement from inside. Was he still asleep? Should I wake him, or just leave the tins for him? I told myself not to be stupid, of course I should wake him. What sort of friend would come all the way out here then sneak away without saying anything?

The new canvas of Jack's tent stood out from the others, which were faded and stained red with dirt. It was tightly closed, which was odd after such a hot night. Jack's pick, shovel and panning dish were stacked neatly outside, but I couldn't hear a sound from inside the tent, not even breathing. I put down the sack of tins and looked in through an eyelet hole in the laced-up flap. Jack was not there. His bed-roll was spread out, a crumpled sheet thrown on top, but there was no sign of Jack.

⁂

'Are you well, Clara?' Mrs Finnerty asked as I went about my work, wiping down their washstand and cleaning out the water bowl.

'Yes, thank you, Mrs Finnerty,' I said, looking up at her worried face.

'It has been so hot, and you do look a bit flushed. I thought you might be suffering from heat stroke.'

'Oh, no, I'm perfectly well,' I smiled at her. 'I just took a longer walk than usual this morning, that's all. It will be hot again today. Is there anything I can get for you from the cooler?'

'It's sweet of you to offer, Clara, but I have my fan and I shall be staying indoors writing letters for most of the day.'

I finished the Finnertys' rooms and went to the kitchen to help Mrs Fagan with the lunch, although it was hard to concentrate. Random thoughts of Jack kept popping into my head.

There were not many people moving about and only a few customers for lunch. I was clearing the tables in the dining room when I saw Jack coming out of the general store. I abandoned my work and rushed out onto the street.

'Jack! Wait,' I called. He turned and smiled. I felt my heart lift. 'Oh, Jack, I was worried about you,' I blurted out.

'And I was worried about you,' he said, ushering me into the shade of an awning.

'Why?' I asked.

'Stupid of me,' he said, shaking his head as if to get rid of the thoughts inside. 'Thanks for the tins.' He looked at me with that open, friendly smile and I wanted to hold him and never let him go.

'Are you staying in town?' I asked.

He considered this for a moment. 'Maybe I will,' he said.

'I have to get back to work,' I said. 'But come in for dinner.'

'You obviously think I'm made of money,' Jack laughed, and we waved to each other as I went back to the pub.

# FEBRUARY 1894

One day, when Florrie and I had cleaned up in the kitchen after dinner, we took off our aprons and joined the stayers in the bar. A man pulled a chair into the middle of the room and stood on it.

'Ladies and gentlemen, I am pleased to announce that a ballad of mine has just been published in the newspaper!' he said.

'Ah, away wit' ya,' Padraig called out. 'It never was.'

'Cross me heart and hope to die,' the man shouted. He searched the pocket of his trousers and pulled out a folded page torn from the newspaper. 'There ya go.' He shook out the folds and waved it in the air. Padraig reached up and snatched it from him. He smoothed the paper, stared at it, and began to read:

*She laughed, and shook her sunny head –*
*Laughter from gates of rose and pearl.*

*'Look in the cook-book, Dan,' she said,*
*'To kiss you first must catch your girl.'*

'Well, I'll be …' Padraig passed the paper across to Jack. I read over his shoulder. The poem was about a woman who flirted with 'Dan' after he had asked her for a kiss. She teased him into following her on horseback for miles and miles, leading him out into very rough country. Each time he came close to catching up with her, she would turn and laugh at him, then gallop away again. She sped away, but fell from her horse and was fatally injured. The last two lines of the poem stayed in my mind:

*He stooped to catch her last faint breath …*
*'You've – caught me – won't you – kiss me – Dan?'*

※

Later that night, Jack and I strolled out to the rocky outcrop. Jack sat down and leaned back on both elbows, his face tilted up to the stars. I sat beside him, thinking about the poem in the bar and the conversation I'd had with Florrie after the Boxing Day ball.

'Jack,' I said, 'have you ever kissed anyone?'

Jack sat up, straightening his arms and resting his hands on the rock. 'My mother,' he said, his mouth twitching up at the corners.

I slapped him on the arm and said, 'You know what I mean!'

He looked serious then. 'No,' he said. 'Why are you asking me that?'

'We are such good friends,' I told him. It was the first

time I had ever felt shy with him, but I had to go on. 'I was just wondering what it would be like – to kiss someone, I mean.'

Jack leaned in close and I shut my eyes. His warm breath was on my cheek. The comforting smell of leather and horses that I always associated with him was strong in my nose. I stayed very still and waited for the sensation of his lips touching mine. Suddenly he shrieked and leapt away from me.

'Oww!' he cried.

My eyes sprang open and I saw him slapping at his hand, blowing on his fingers and stomping one foot down hard on the rock. I leapt up, too, not knowing what to expect – a snake, a goanna, a spiny devil? I saw nothing that could have caused him such distress.

'What is it?' I asked.

He lifted his foot and we both bent down to see what it was that he'd squashed under his boot.

'A bull ant!' I cried and jumped further back. 'Oh, Jack, there will be others.' I began to search for them, bending low to examine the surface of the rock, the sandy soil around it. 'Let's get away from here,' I said.

'Clara,' Jack looked at me quizzically. 'It's dead now.'

'I don't care. This one may be dead, but where are the others? I can't stand bull ants!' I shrieked.

Jack began to laugh.

'It's not funny, Jack Raeside. Stop laughing.' Of course, that only made him laugh even more.

'I don't believe it,' he said. 'You can't be scared of a bull ant! I've seen you stare down a huge bungarra, and patch up a man with a bullet hole in his chest. You're not even afraid of Mrs Fagan and she scares the pants off most people!'

Suddenly I saw how ridiculous I must seem, and felt ashamed. Jack looked confused.

'Are you disappointed in me, Jack?' My voice came out small and childish.

He shook his head. 'Come here,' he said, and held me in his arms.

# FEBRUARY 1894

Florrie left Coolgardie as she had arrived – on Snell's coach. We hugged each other and I told her, for the hundredth time, that I wished she would stay. She shook her head.

'Where will you go?' I asked, a deep sadness weighing me down.

'I don't really know,' she said. 'But I fancy somewhere cooler. Maybe I'll work in Perth for a while.'

'Write to me,' I pleaded.

'I will.'

She waved as Mr Snell shook the reins and called to his horses. The coach moved off towards the west.

Everyone had come to see her off. Jack, Mrs Fagan, Mr Wisdom, Arthur Williams, even the Finnertys. We had all grown to love her.

'Will she come back, do you think? Jack asked.

'I don't know. She says not.'

'Lucky I'm here then,' Jack said.

After the dance that evening we took the north-east track out of town for about two miles. Sandgroper was away to the right, in a patch of mallee scrub. From the top of a rise, we could see Jack's tent. At first, I thought he was taking me there. My heart beat a little faster, but the tent had been closed up all day and would be unbearably hot inside. The wind came fitfully across the desert, not yet blowing a gale as it would later, but moving the air enough to give some relief from the heat of the day. The distinctive smell of the camp wafted towards us. A mixture of wood smoke, canvas and latrines.

Jack placed a hand on my arm. 'Shh,' he whispered. A shadowy shape flickered around his tent – pale, elongated, there one minute and gone the next. In the moonlight I saw pointed ears, a long snout, a tail carried low.

'Bloody dingo,' Jack said, as it disappeared over the ridge on the far side of the camp.

'Oh, Jack, has it been raiding your stores again?'

'I hope not,' he said. 'I've put lids on everything and sealed up the bottom of the tent with rocks.'

'Should we go and see?'

'No, too late to save anything now,' he said. 'Come on, let's just enjoy being cool.'

*

Later, outside my door, Jack leaned in close to my ear. 'Sleep tight, don't let the bed bugs bite,' he said softly.

I dug him in the ribs with my elbow. 'What bed bugs?' I asked. 'I'm in charge of beds around here. How dare you suggest there are bugs in them!' He stepped back and rubbed his ribs, but I could see that he was laughing, silently, so as not to wake Mrs Fagan. He crossed the yard. At the corner of the building he turned and waved. I waved and blew him a kiss to make up for the sore ribs.

# FEBRUARY 1894

In the morning I slept a little later than usual. I was in the kitchen with my tea and toast when Mr Wisdom came in.

'Warden Finnerty wants to see you, Clara. He's waiting in my office,' Mr Wisdom said. I wondered why, but I had a mouthful of toast and couldn't ask. Thinking that the Finnertys must need fresh towels in their room, I finished my tea, wiped my hands on my apron, and went to speak to him.

The warden was standing in the tiny room, which had been partitioned off from the dining room. He was looking out through the narrow window, roughly cut into the wall to let in some light. He turned when he heard me come in.

'Ah, Clara,' he said, and indicated a chair that belonged in the dining room. It didn't feel right to sit down before he did, but he insisted. I watched him pace the small room several times. He stopped and stood in front of me.

'I'm so sorry to have to do this, Clara, but I need to interview you,' he said. I waited, wondering why he was being so formal.

'Were you with Jack last night?'

'Yes,' I said. 'At the dance.'

'And after the dance?'

'We went for a stroll, out towards the Sandgroper.'

He nodded. 'Did you and Jack have an argument?'

'No. Why would we?'

'I believe you had a falling out … in the pub the other day.' His eyes held mine and I felt confused. Had I done something wrong? Mr Finnerty was very precise about the law, but he had often said to me that he trusted my judgement.

He turned his back, took a few steps towards the window, then came and sat down again. Resting his hand on my arm he said, 'There is no easy way to tell you this, Clara. Jack was found dead this morning.'

I stared at him. Then I smiled and shook my head.

'No, that can't be right,' I said. 'There's some mistake. Jack walked home with me about midnight. He'll be sleeping in his tent, that's all.'

'I'm afraid there is no mistake.' The warden was looking at me with such a deep sadness in his eyes that, even as my voice denied it, I felt my body folding in on itself, slumping into the chair.

'No!' I said again. The warden waited. Suddenly I could not sit there any longer. I jumped up, knocking the chair aside. 'Where is he? I want to see him,' I demanded.

'I'm sorry, Clara, but I don't think that would be a good idea.'

'Why not?'

The warden hesitated. He righted my chair. Then he drew in a deep breath and said, 'Because it would be better for you to remember him the way he was – when you last saw him.'

I sat down heavily. This can't be happening, I thought. Jack is alive. Of course he is. He will be having a good laugh at all of us thinking otherwise. He's probably gone off to do some prospecting, or to visit Padraig at Tipperary.

'Please, I need to see Jack,' I said. 'If he's not in his camp, I can probably find him.'

'We have found him,' Warden Finnerty said. As the silence lengthened between us, a terrible certainty crept into my soul.

'Why can I not see him, then?' I said in a very small voice that did not seem to belong to me.

'It will only cause you more pain,' the warden said, pacing again.

'But I have to see Jack.' I took a step towards the door, but the warden stood blocking my way. When I tried to dodge around him he caught hold of my wrist and held it tight.

'Jack was found dead on the ridge outside town,' he said. 'With a rifle beside him. His face has been blown off.'

My hands flew to my own face. I heard a cry of anguish, an injured animal sound that at first I didn't recognise, but my mouth was open, my head flung back. I tasted salt in the corner of my mouth. Hot tears were pooling there. I leapt to my feet. 'I want to see him!' I shouted. 'I want to see Jack!'

Then Mrs Fagan was there. She placed a mug of hot tea on the desk beside me. A strong smell of brandy rose up with the steam. 'Drink this, pet,' she said gently. I stared at the mug as if it would bite me. Then I swept it onto the floor and fled.

# FEBRUARY 1894

The desert wind cut like a knife. I shouted into it defiantly. Great cries of anguish came out of my mouth, wrenched from the deepest part of my being. Ghastly sounds that flew shrieking into the vast, empty spaces of the land and died there. The shifting sands absorbed them. Rocks, flecked with fool's gold, scattered them, and hid them amongst the bones of other dead things. 'Jack! Jack! Wait! Don't go without me.'

I must have been making plans, not even knowing I did so, never really doubting that my life and Jack's would always be linked. One minute I was angry with him for being so careless. Because it had to have been an accident. He wouldn't leave me like that on purpose, and who could want to hurt Jack? The next minute I was furious with myself for never saying the most important things to him. The future had been swept up and thrown away, discarded in the empty shafts, the 'white man's holes' of Coolgardie.

What use was a king's ransom? All the gold in the world would not buy one more moment of time for me and Jack. I turned my head to one side, then the other, looking for some way forward. Even with my eyes wide open I could not see anything but emptiness. My head began to turn more quickly, from side to side, until I was shaking it like a dog with a flea in his ear, desperately trying to dislodge the unwanted truth.

Finally exhausted, I slumped down on the sand.

⁂

Sometime later I became conscious of a human presence. I lifted my head. An Aboriginal woman with a baby on her hip stood looking down at me. I got slowly to my feet. She did not move, but stood regarding me steadily with her large black eyes. The naked baby stared at me with its matching black eyes.

'You bin sleep long time, missus,' the woman said at last.

I looked up at the sun and saw that it was well past midday. The sky was bleached almost white. There was not a cloud anywhere to cast a cooling shadow on the parched land. I shook red dirt off my skirt and tugged at my apron. It was crumpled and stained with tears.

'Lallie,' the woman said. I tried to speak, but my mouth was dry and I couldn't get my tongue to work. 'Lallie,' she said again, placing one hand on the bones of her chest above her bare breasts.

I moved my tongue over cracked lips. 'Clara,' I said.

She nodded. 'Come.'

Other, more distant voices came softly at first, then more urgently, and I shifted my gaze in their direction.

Three women and several children stood in a group about fifty yards away, watching us. Lallie beckoned and they slowly came closer, eyes lowered.

'Come,' Lallie urged, and started to walk. The sun blazed down. My skin felt tight, sunburnt. I looked around for any sort of landmark that would tell me where I was. In my anguish I had broken the first rule of this unforgiving land. I had not given a single thought to my surroundings, or to checking my direction. There was nothing I recognised. Without Lallie I would be hopelessly lost. I hurried after her.

Lallie moved effortlessly over the sand while I stumbled along behind. The sun beat down on my unprotected head. My dry eyes squinted against the glare.

Lallie stopped and pointed. At first, I could see nothing but low, sandy ridges, blown by the wind to form ripples on a blood-red sea. Lallie pointed again. Away in the distance, scoured into the plain, were two straight lines, starkly white against the red-brown country. They could only be the tracks of many wheels.

'Thank you,' I said, and held out my hand to Lallie. With a slight nod of her head she hitched the baby higher on her hip and walked away. 'Thank you,' I called after her.

❊

It was mid-afternoon, but there was no-one in the kitchen when I reached the hotel. I heard voices in the dining room and hesitated in the adjoining doorway.

'Clara!' Mrs Fagan saw me first. 'There ya are, pet! Come and have a cup of tea.' I didn't move, but looked at them in turn.

‘We were worried about you,’ Mr Wisdom said gently.

‘I’m sorry,’ I said.

‘Are you all right?’ Arthur Williams looked at my dishevelled hair, my sunburnt face. Then he went behind the bar and lifted a bottle of brandy from the shelf.

‘Thank ya, Arthur.’ Mrs Fagan took the bottle from him, put her other arm around my shoulder and ushered me into the kitchen.

Mrs Fagan poured tea into two mugs and laced them both with brandy. We sat together in silence, sipping the strong, sweet liquid. When I had drained my mug, Mrs Fagan offered me more.

‘No, thank you,’ I said. She poured another mug of tea for herself and seemed in no hurry to go on with the work, which I was feeling guilty about. But I didn’t move. My legs felt weak and shaky. I wanted to go on sitting there, safe in the kitchen, with the familiar sounds of the hotel going about its usual business, and the solid presence of Mrs Fagan sitting opposite.

‘Do you know an Aboriginal woman called Lallie, Mrs Fagan?’ I asked, wanting to keep her there just a little longer.

‘Can’t say I do,’ Mrs Fagan replied. ‘I do think it’s a shame, what’s happenin’ to them. It’s our fault, mind. Ya can’t expect them to keep themselves healthy when camels foul their waterholes and the dams and soaks are so dry.’

‘I say the same thing to Jack – said the same thing.’ I looked at Mrs Fagan, who reached across the table and patted my hand. ‘Lallie showed me the way home today,’ I said.

‘’Twas kind of her, so it was,’ Mrs Fagan said. ‘No doubt she went out of her way.’

'I had not wanted to be brought back. I had wanted to be with Jack.' I knew I was not making any sense, but I wanted to say more, as if words would bring back some certainty to the world, if only I could produce enough of them. Mrs Fagan sat listening, nodding occasionally, until no more words came. Then she covered my hand with hers.

'Come now,' she said and stood up. She took my arm and walked with me to my room. I clung to her and she helped me into bed. My eyes were already closing when she leaned down and said softly, 'Nothin' will ever be the same as yer first love, pet. But ya're here, and Jack is not. Think on it, so.'

⁂

The next morning I woke with grit in my mouth and puffy eyes. I got up and washed my face, rinsed out my mouth, being careful not to swallow any of the water from the bowl, and dressed in clean clothes. My mind was numb, but I felt the need to be moving around, doing things, anything that kept me busy and stopped me from thinking too much. It was still early, but I went to the kitchen. The new batch of dough had risen overnight and everything was neat and in its place. I wondered how long Mrs Fagan had had to stay up working, on her own, to make it that way, and felt a rush of gratitude for her unquestioning support.

I stirred the coals in the kitchen fire and added the last of the wood from the box next to the hearth. The box needed refilling so I carried it out to the woodheap at the back of the shed. As always, the brushwood had been sorted, cut into different lengths and neatly stacked according to size. I filled the box and carried it back to the kitchen. The sun was not yet up and the kitchen was still dim. As I stepped through the door a figure came towards me. It was Jack's friend Bill Lockhart.

'Hello, Bill,' I said, but didn't look at him. I knew he would speak about Jack. My feelings were still too raw, my thoughts too confused. I didn't know what to say, so I hid my face by bending over and carefully putting the box down beside the hearth.

'Terrible … what happened to Jack,' Bill said quietly

I straightened up slowly to face him. 'Yes,' I said.

'I have to tell you, just so you know.'

'Know what?'

'That Jack's death was an accident. A freak accident. There's no way it could have been anything else.'

I stared at Bill then, shocked that anyone could possibly have thought otherwise. 'What are you saying?' I asked.

'Nothing! Well, no, that's not quite true. Warden Finnerty has to investigate any sudden or suspicious death. And you were the last person to see Jack alive.'

The rifle, long forgotten in the corner, seemed to leap out at me. My legs buckled. Bill rushed to my side and helped me to a chair.

'The last person … Is he saying …?' I couldn't go on. Did they think I killed Jack? Even Warden Finnerty? My head felt as if it didn't belong to me. I laid my arms on the table and rested my head on them.

'I'll make you some tea,' Bill said. He put more wood on the fire and moved the kettle to the middle of the hotplate. When it came to the boil, he swilled out the teapot and tipped the last of yesterday's cold tea and spent leaves onto the straggling mint plant. Mrs Fagan was determined to grow mint in a pot, just outside the door. 'To keep away the flies,' she always said, but it never did.

'You know that a dingo had been raiding Jack's camp,' Bill began, spooning fresh tea-leaves from the caddy into the pot.

'Yes,' I said, lifting my aching head. 'But Jack had dealt with it. He had put his flour in a barrel and everything else in tins with lids.'

'Them dingos don't give up easy,' Bill said, shaking his head slowly. 'I heard Jack come back to his tent after the dance. There was a lot of swearing and sounds of Jack moving around. Then he went somewhere. Padraig says Jack had borrowed his rifle earlier. Said he was going to sort out the pesky bugger once and for all.' Bill lifted his mug of tea and blew across the top of it. 'There was a big moon that night,' he continued. 'But you know that.'

Immediately my mind leapt back. I saw the feldspar glinting in the rock, and heard Jack's voice. I saw him smiling and tried to block out a sudden image of his face damaged beyond recognition. I swallowed hard to stop the tears from escaping. 'Some of the fellas, the ones who weren't too drunk, they say they heard a shot, but they thought nothin' of it. In the mornin' though … Well, you know the rest.'

'I don't! No-one will tell me! They won't let me see him. I need to see him, Bill.' My voice was shaking and the tears were streaming down my face, soaking the front of my blouse. I mopped at them angrily.

Bill stood up and came around to my side of the table. He put his hand on my shoulder and said, 'They've taken him away, Clara. Warden Finnerty had the body removed.'

I blew my nose, and tried to compose myself. 'Please, Bill, I need to know what happened.'

Bill hesitated, but he understood. 'It's obvious that Jack was after the dingo,' he began. 'He was climbing up the ridge, probably to get a better look, or to take a shot. The marks are still there, where his boots slipped on the loose stones. He must have fallen and the rifle in his hand went off.' Bill turned his face towards the door and took a deep breath. 'In the mornin', when I went outside to have a leak, I noticed somethin' on the ridge. At first, I didn't want to look, but I had to be sure.' He tipped his mug and drained the tea from it. 'He didn't suffer, Clara, I'm certain of it. He might have heard the bang. That's all.' Bill stared into his empty mug, avoiding my eyes. 'Padraig is blamin' himself, for lendin' Jack the rifle, and … Well, I should have got up when I heard him leave his tent.'

'Will you take me out there, Bill?' I said at last.

'Jack's not there,' Bill said. 'There's nothin' left.'

'I know. But I want to see where Jack died,' I pleaded. 'You found him. You can show me the exact spot.' I caught hold of Bill's hand and held it tightly, as if I was drowning and he was my last hope of rescue. The first rays of the sun sent a shaft of light into the room and I looked into Bill's eyes. There was hurt there. He shuffled his feet, obviously reluctant, perhaps as much for his own sake as mine. But I could not let go of him until he agreed to take me.

'Okay,' he said at last. 'But it's about a mile out.' I stared at him. 'Sorry, I was forgettin' you walk further than that most mornin's.'

'If I had to walk a hundred miles, I would still want to go,' I told him.

# FEBRUARY 1894

Just on sunset, Bill came around to the back door to find me. I was ready.

We set off towards the ridge with the last rays of the sun striking gold on the tips of the Reward Reef. The stamps at Bayley's Mine were still smashing down on the red-brown rocks, each crushing blow sending a shudder through the earth.

We walked silently, both engrossed in our own thoughts. Before long, a strong smell of excrement filled the air. Clouds of flies rose up. They crawled all over me, into the corners of my eyes and mouth, even down the neck of my blouse. Bill was just ahead of me. His back was covered in a moving mass of black insects. Like me, he constantly swept his hands in front of his face and looked down to avoid stepping in the worst of the mess underfoot.

At last we reached the base of the ridge. Tents were pitched in clusters on the other side, sheltering from the full force of the wind that blew from the east. The smell here was less of excrement and more of rancid fat and cooking fires. My stomach turned over and bitter bile rose in my throat. I clamped my mouth shut. The horror of swallowing another live fly was stronger than the urge to vomit.

Bill began to climb ahead of me. The slope was covered in loose stones. My boots slipped. I flung out my hands to save myself. The rocks tore at my fingernails and grazed my palms.

Near the highest point, where the ridge was steepest, Bill stopped. There were dark patches where blood had soaked into the ground. Jack's blood. The scrape marks from his boots showed where he had slipped and fallen. I dropped to my knees and picked up a stone. A thick coating of dried blood covered its surface. I held it to my cheek. It felt warm from being in the sun. I picked up two more bloodied stones and put them in the pocket of my apron.

Bill was looking at me strangely.

'This is all I have left of him,' I said.

⁂

In the dark days that followed, I would sometimes find myself standing still, on the verandah, or in one of the rooms. I would have a pile of sheets in my arms, or a dust cloth in my hand, not knowing whether I had just finished the cleaning, or whether I was about to begin. How long had I been standing there? A few minutes? Half an hour? I had no idea.

Arthur Williams found me like this one day.

'Clara? Are you ill?' he said. 'You look very pale.'

'What?' I hadn't heard his footsteps, even on the creaky wooden boards. 'No, I'm not ill.' Although I suppose it was a sort of illness. For no reason I would suddenly feel overwhelmed. My mind would go blank and, without warning, my body would stop moving. The emptiness inside me expanded, growing until it consumed everything: my past, my present, my future. I found it very hard to laugh, or even smile.

'Take a few days off, Clara,' Mr Wisdom suggested.

'Oh, no. I couldn't do that,' I told him. 'Mrs Fagan needs me. And the Finnertys. I have already let them down.'

'It's all right. They understand,' he said.

I shook my head.

# MARCH 1894

Perhaps a month had gone by since Jack died. I carried out my usual tasks, but time had lost all meaning for me. Mr Wisdom called me into his office.

'Sit down, Clara.' He indicated the same chair that I had sat in when Warden Finnerty told me about Jack. It was as if the clock had turned back, but not far enough. At the moment when I last sat in this chair Jack was already dead, although I didn't know it then. If only I could make time go back further. To the dance, to Jack holding me in his arms, smiling at me and making jokes. If I could go back to that night I would never leave him. I would sleep in his tent, scare off the dingo, poison it with cyanide from the mine. Jack would never borrow that rifle. Together we would think of something else, find another way to keep everything safe. It was only when Mr Wisdom handed me his handkerchief that I noticed the tears running down my cheeks.

'I was wondering if you would like to work in the bar,' he said. 'Just for a couple of hours in the afternoons, when most of the men are out working. If you could do that for me, I could get my ordering done.' I looked blankly at him, not knowing what to say. 'It might cheer you up a bit. You have become very quiet, Clara. You don't smile anymore.'

I agreed to try the job in the bar and found it was good to be with people again. The shiftworkers who came in the afternoons were funny, lively, loud and full of outrageous stories. For the whole of my two hours each day my mind and my body were fully occupied. There was always someone telling a joke, or reciting a poem from the *Bulletin*. I was making a collection of poems from the literary section of the paper, cutting them out and pasting them into my exercise book. They were definitely not Shakespeare, but the ballads were told with such dry wit, and a rough, earthy humour that made me laugh.

I especially loved the sad poems. They spoke to the sadness in me and I felt that at least there were others in the world who understood the heaviness I carried in my heart.

The evenings were the hardest. Sometimes I caught myself hurrying through the last of my chores, thinking 'Jack will be waiting', or stepped out onto the verandah expecting to see him leaning against the wall. The disappointment of finding he was not there would hit me like a physical blow. I had to rush into my room, shut out the world and climb into bed.

I took to writing in my exercise book again. I mostly wrote about Jack, about our time together, sometimes laughing at his funny ways as I scribbled on the page; at other times dropping tears onto the paper, making it crinkle as the sea had once done.

*I know that a part of me will always be missing. Jack took it with him and I want him to keep it*, I wrote.

# ABOUT CLARA

Clara Saunders went on to outlive three husbands.

Arthur Williams was the first. He had been in love with Clara from the start, but knew that, after Jack's death, he must try not to rush her. Instead he made himself indispensable, fetching things, repairing her shoes, bringing in wood for the stove.

Four months passed. Clara turned sixteen and Arthur organised a birthday party for her. Afterwards, when everyone else had gone, he proposed to her. She was shocked, but said she would think about it.

At first Clara didn't have a lot to say to Arthur, but he talked enough for both of them. He told her about a new field opening up ninety miles to the north of Coolgardie. He had plans to start up a hotel and billiard room of his own.

Before their wedding on 4 July 1894, Arthur travelled to the city. He took with him the nugget that Paddy Hannan had given to Clara and had it made into a brooch as a wedding present. Clara wore it pinned to her wedding dress.

Just a few weeks later, Clara and Arthur moved to the Ninety Mile, which would later become Goongarrie township, and set up their first hotel there. Within a year, she and Arthur bought another hotel at Mount Morgans and moved again. They had two daughters, Lillian Mary (1896) and Violet Catherine (1898). Sadly, Arthur died of pneumonia while he was in England visiting his aged aunts who, having no children of their own, wanted him to inherit the family property.

Clara sent the girls to boarding school in Perth and stayed on to run the hotel, on her own, for seven years. After her marriage to John Joseph Lynch, Clara left the goldfields in 1910, and became a pioneer of the wheatbelt with her second husband. They had two boys, John Leopold (1909) and Edward Joseph (1910). In 1939, tragedy struck again when John Joseph Lynch died of a heart attack while working on the farm. Clara moved to Perth and lived with her sister, Susan, who had also been widowed. In 1944 Clara married John Paton.

Clara Paton (nee Saunders) was seventy-seven years old when she died, in 1956, from complications after a cataract operation. Not long before her death, Clara's granddaughter noticed that she was often writing in an old exercise book. When she asked Clara what she was writing, her grandmother told her it was just old memories.

You can find more information on Clara and on life in the Western Australian goldfields on my website: elaineforrestal.com.au

Teaching notes are available on the Fremantle Press website: fremantlepress.com.au

# ACKNOWLEDGEMENTS

We are lucky, in Western Australia, to have Cate Sutherland, Children's Publisher at Fremantle Press, and her multi-talented team. Without them, Clara's story would still be languishing in the archives of the J.S. Battye Library. Special thanks to Armelle Davies for guiding me through the minefield of electronic editing and to my friends and colleagues at The Literature Centre, SCBWI and the Children's Book Council of Australia for providing support and stimulation.

I wish also to thank Jan James, sadly no longer with us, and Ambelin Kwaymullina for their advice and for directing me to comprehensive references regarding Aboriginal protocols early in the drafting of the manuscript.

On pages 185–186, I have included some lines from the bush ballad 'At the Diggings Store' by R.A.F., first published in the *Bulletin* in 1896. Although this poem was published after the events of this novel, I felt that it was important to include. It is an example of the way in which bush poets captured that particular brand of wry humour, quiet courage and mateship displayed by the men of the time, who lived in such harsh conditions on the Coolgardie goldfields where, sadly, death was a common occurrence.

First published 2020 by
FREMANTLE PRESS

This edition first published 2025.

Fremantle Press Inc. trading as Fremantle Press
PO Box 158, North Fremantle, Western Australia, 6159
fremantlepress.com.au



Cover design by Rebecca Mills, rebeccamills.com.au
Cover illustration by Briony Stewart
Printed by Everbest Printing Investment Limited, China

NATIONAL LIBRARY OF AUSTRALIA
A catalogue record for this book is available from the National Library of Australia

ISBN 9781760994969 (paperback)
ISBN 9781760994976 (ebook)

GOVERNMENT OF WESTERN AUSTRALIA
Department of Local Government, Sport and Cultural Industries
lotterywest

Fremantle Press is supported by the State Government through the Department of Local Government, Sport and Cultural Industries.

Fremantle Press respectfully acknowledges the Whadjuk people of the Noongar nation as the Traditional Owners and Custodians of the land where we work in Walyalup.

FSC www.fsc.org
MIX
From responsible sources
FSC® C124385